GIRL F?CK HIM

D1548020

BY

CRISANN SMITH

COPYRIGHT

ACKNOWLEDGEMENTS

Pop You Shit Sis

I first want to acknowledge the outstanding debt I owe to Blaq Bailey. I could have never finished this process without you. You have supported me through the doubt—my right hand when mine felt weak. My cheerleader when I wasn't winning the game and the kind of best friend every girl should have. I share this "Victory Lap" with you.

DEDICATION

Thank you, God, for trusting me to be the messenger. I take no credit, only honor that you have chosen me. No matter how hard this journey became, you graced me with peace through the transition. I could never repay you. You've already paid it all. And I Thank You for each person you've sent along this journey to make it all possible. Thank You, Father, for being who you are even when I'm not being who I'm called to be. You are the real MVP!

I want to thank my momma Kathy Smith and my daughter Skylar Smith. You are both the loves of my life. Every day is for you. Thank you, family and friends, for everything you have contributed to me. Rather through conversation, your service, or simply praying for me. Too many of you to name, but you know who you are. I would like you to know that I am grateful for you.

Now let's get into this all-woman production -

Author: CrisAnn Smith

Book Cover Design: CrisAnn Smith

Book Cover Formatting: Rose Miller

Publisher: C. A. Smith Enterprises LLC (CrisAnn Smith)

Management: Emily (Blaq) Bailey

Digital Marketing: Eluminer Digital (Dianne Robinson) / Emily (Blaq) Bailey

Editor/Formatting: TSG LaReka Bailey

Editor/Formatting: Emmany Clair

Photographer: 928 Studios (Veronica Gordon)

Thank You, Ladies, for making my visions a reality. The power behind a woman is unmeasured. I was told to change this and this. Do that and that before someone would publish me. This dream team came together and said, "Fuck that, and them," we can do this on our own... And "WE" did. Job well-done, ladies!

Lastly, thank you to each person who has played a role in my success. Good or bad, you counted me out BUT I made it!

Table of Contents

CHAPTER 1

INTRODUCTION

I've had time to process who the fuck I really am. I'm nothing like people perceive me to be. My life has been nothing but a complete fairytale, a fairytale of what society says it should be. Rude awakening; life happened, and it happened fast, fun, funny, and fabulous. Fortunately, I stopped asking for permission and made my own fucking rules! I dated who I wanted, fucked who I wanted, said no when I wanted, but most importantly, made my money how the fuck I wanted. I once took on the role of perfect Patty and tried to please everyone around me. Yet I had no idea who I really was until I met Eric. He changed, groomed, and stretched me into the Reece I am today. Eric instantly grabbed my attention with his well-groomed demeanor, charming personality, and articulate conversation. He stood, about 6'3 with dimples, dark hair with a taper fade, and deep waves with a perfectly edged goatee. When I met Eric, his scent was ''1 Million Paco Rabanne'' cologne, dressed in a tailored Tom Ford suit and custom RI Notti shoes, with a smile to make any woman graciously hand over her panties (Oh, and I did). Not to mention, the dick is hung like a King Cobra. WHEW CHILE!

Enough about me for now; let's talk about these friends of mine: Olivia, Mia, Chloe, and of course, Ava. Some consider us as the dream team or the bitches from hell. Either way, we leave an unforgettable taste in your mouth, sweet or sour. It's funny how we all met and formed a lasting friendship through the hurt, disappointments, disagreements, babies, work, and life happenings. We only grew closer and bonded together.

Olivia and I have been friends since high school into our Spelman College days, Ava and I met at work, Mia and Chloe are my neighbors. Olivia (Livy), my high yellow know-it-all friend, is my certified secret keeper and baby momma. She is an exceptional mother to my goddaughter, Ryan Nychole, named after me. Livy and I have been friends for 20-plus years. I honestly can't imagine life without her, except when she's being a complete control freak, and did I mention "know it all?" I remember when we once sat outside my ex-boyfriend's house all night, stalking him to confirm what I already knew. He was cheating! Of course, I still stayed with him for another fucking two years, subjecting myself to more pain. Such a foolish girl in love, with the idea of love, not knowing what love really was at the time. Livy and I are employed at one of the top Law Firms in Texas where I currently hold the Chief Executive of Operations position, and Livy is on the legal team as one of the lead attorneys.

Ava, my sweet, sweet Ava, works as the Executive Assistant to the legal team at the same firm as Livy and me. She is nothing short of amazing. When I think of Ava, I think of butterflies: colorful, free, and beautiful. Her smooth chocolate skin, long caramel highlighted hair, and paper white teeth remind me of a creme brûlée latte freshly steamed with fat-free milk. I randomly met Ava at the detail spa, not knowing we work for the same law firm two floors apart. I complimented her 2000 chameleon color 718 Cayman Porsche, and the rest is history. She has the energy of brand-new Prada shoes on the red carpet of a movie premiere; she is sassy as fuck!

A few years ago, I bought my first home. It was one of the most accomplished moments in my life. I purchased it in the community I've been eyeing for years, The Weatherford Estates on the Lake. I thought I wouldn't ever own a home in this neighborhood, but I'm so grateful that I do. I wouldn't have met Mia and Chloe. Mia and Ray (Mia's husband) live across the street from me. My first encounter with Mia and Ray was me yelling across the street, "keep your fucking dog off my lawn!" Mia is a stay-at-home mom. She is a calm spirit, classy, and very soft-spoken. She gives comfort and positive vibes in any situation. Ray, on the other hand, is an utter asshole! His arrogance and superior attitude remind me of "The Joker," a straight-up clown. Oh, I failed to mention he has the body of a Greek God, sun-kissed flawless skin with an Italian accent, and yes, he is a black man. I will not take away from how I view him as a father. He is fantastic with the boys. Brendan (2) and Bryant (4) years of age are a joy to be around, full of energy and life. However, as a husband, that's a whole other story; and this book doesn't have enough chapters.

Ms. Chloe Jackson – Dr. C.J is what they call her – I call her big fine. She is 5'9 with a body you dream about, built, not bought. She gives African warrior vibes with her tasseled dreadlocks, perfectly arched eyebrows, melanin-rich skin, and breathtaking smile. Her presence is so strong that it's often mistaken for attitude. It's merely a woman who knows who she is and what she possesses. It's called confidence and self-love. My next-door neighbor and OBGYN is the epitome of a diva. She will give you her truths and never back down from a debate or fight. She is my shoot first, ask questions later friend; every girl should have one of those friends.

One Sunday morning on the way to church, we were running a tad bit late, per usual, when CJ was the driver. We finally arrived at the church, and we were looking for parking. "I see a spot," CJ stated. She turned on her blinker to signal that she was about to pull into that parking spot. In the blink of an eye, another car swooped in and got into the parking spot before us. She quickly pulled behind the car, and I knew it was about to go down. CJ rolled down her window and yelled out to the lady who was getting out of the car, "didn't you see me about to park there?" The lady said excuse me, with a roll of her neck. Oh shit, I went mute. CJ then put her car in park, opened the door, and said, "Bitch, if you don't move this car, you're going to meet the Lord sooner than later!" This is only one of many instances with the diva herself. It's never a dull moment.

Oh, and by the way, I'm Sharice Ryan, and who's better than me to tell my story?

CHAPTER 2

REECE

Hi Andy, can I get my usual, a Venti green tea light ice and a Grande black coffee, please? As I reach for my wallet, my phone rings, and it's my favorite notification, Eric! I answered in a slightly seductive tone, yet very pleasant and posed.

"Good Morning, handsome man!" He replies intriguingly, "Good Morning, sunflower! How is your morning coming along?" With the biggest grin on my face, I responded, "it's much better now that I get to hear your voice. When am I going to see you? I desperately miss your face, your lips, your smell, and your touch." He giggled and said, "I'm coming back into town this week. Let's get together this weekend." With no hesitation, I quickly responded, "Great! I'll book us a room at the Ritz-Carlton Hotel for a change in scenery, a mini getaway. Would Saturday evening work for you, my love?"

"Yes, Saturday is good. I was just calling to wish you a good day. I just made it to my meeting. I'll check in with you a little later on Reesie Pieces." As much as I hated to end that 5-seconds phone call, I sucked up my disappointment and said, "okay, have a productive meeting and an awesome day. We'll talk later." I love it when he calls me Reesie Pieces. Hell, let's be honest, I love whatever he calls me, as long as he's calling, making me a priority in his busy life.

Eric and I met at a corporate fundraiser for under privilege children in our community. Eric is considered to be a real estate mogul. He is an entrepreneur who has built a massive real estate empire worldwide. A true boss and entrepreneur, my type of guy. When he first approached me, I pretended that I was uninterested and unbothered, knowing damn well that every other woman in the building and I was eyeing him and knew exactly who he was. Yet, he sought after me, and shit, why wouldn't he? I am that bitch.

After he formally introduced himself to me, we stood there talking and laughing the rest of the night. We hit it off so well that it felt as if we had been friends for years, but there was this one thing that almost got his ass canceled. Although we talked all night after meeting at the auction, this mother-fucker had the audacity to not call me until two weeks later. The fuck! He tried it! I bet he never tries that shit again. Finally, after a few rounds of phone tag, unanswered voicemails, and open-ended text messages, he got the drift – quickly!

He redeemed himself with an invitation to breakfast. That grand gesture grabbed my attention, or maybe it was the presentation of the invite that captured me. Most men ask you to dinner so that (A) he tries to get you to come back to his place or (B) tries to find reasons to come back to your place. Either way, the shit is lame as fuck and definitely won't fly with me. So instead, Eric invited me to a quaint and yet chic Haitian-style cafe for breakfast.

This place was full of so much charm and history. The walls were filled with famous historical black men and women. Someone distinctly hung portraits of Madam CJ Walker along with graphic drawings of poet Amanda Gorman and so on. The food was incredible, and the chef was a black woman.

I asked him how did he find this hidden gem? He then began to express his love for black history, black movements, black art, black unity, black power, and, most importantly,

supporting black-owned businesses. Lawd, THIS MAN! His intellect and dialogue had my strawberry screaming, "taste me, eat me now." His assertiveness, charisma, and demeanor are a for sure panty dropper. Yet, as heated and turned on as I was, I kept it cute and ended our morning early with a handshake and an "I hope we will do this again soon." While every thought in my head was about him fucking me and me begging him not to stop, I had to keep my cool and composure.

"Reece, what are you doing? Let's go!" *Ugggggggggggh! Damn Ava!* She knows exactly how to ruin a wet dream.

"I'm coming. Didn't you see me getting my coffee? So what's the hurry to get to the office anyway?"

"Are you kidding me, REECE! You are seriously not that self-absorbed that you forgot the celebration for Liv today for winning that big case for the firm?" *That's today!* "No Bitch, I didn't forget that my best friend of 20 years WOOOOOOOOOOOON the case against Hudson Hudson & Associates, and is being considered for the Senior Partner position! And for the record, I am not that self-absorbed." Lord, help me! I'm a horrible friend. I forgot Livy's celebration. I managed to order and send a flower bouquet, edible arrangements, and summon my little sister to run to the mall to buy Liv something shiny and sparkly, all by the time we made it to the elevators to scream surprise.

The gang is here (Ava, Liv, Mia, and CJ), but why the hell is Ray here? He wasn't the Judge on Liv's case, and Mia didn't need a chaperon. I guess this is a safe place for him to be with his wife since his hoes no longer work at our firm. When I first met Ray, it was inside a courtroom. He was a prominent attorney turned D.A. who blossomed into a State Supreme Court - Appellate Judge.

Somewhere down the line, he forgot he was Raymond Lastra and morphed into Denzel Washington in "Mo Better Blues." I heard Ray's name before I even met him. I heard he was a real ladies' man, minus the wife. He carries himself as a single man when in reality, he is a family man who needs to be repurposed and repackaged. I wasn't trying to become as close as I am with Mia, his wife, but it was hard not to. She's so kind, genuine, and sweet! So many times, I've wanted to tell her all the things I know about Ray, but I don't. I bite my tongue, close my mouth, and move on. The hard truth is she already knows, and I don't want to embarrass her any further than he already has.

"Liv! I'm so proud of you and what you have accomplished! Oh, and bitch, you fucking shit up in that Badgley Mischka suit."

"YAS! Thank You, sister. I am so humbled at this moment."

"Girl, don't do that modest shit with us. I know you are feeling bossy! As you should."

"Yea, I'm feeling real Bey-On-Ce-Ish! I called you last night to tell you about my child's father."

"I meant to call you back; what the hell has he done now?"

"He's always on some bullshit. You know him! He told Ryan that he would not come around anymore since she has a new daddy."

"Liv, please tell me you made this up? Why would he say that to a 4-year-old? Better yet, he didn't have to say shit. He doesn't come around anyway."

"Exactly! I let him have it. I said to that coward-ass nigga, do what you do best and disappear, and don't call my baby anymore till you get your shit together. I told him he should be thankful another man has stepped in and became visible to your daughter since you're a ghost to her!" "Girl, fuck him! What we're not going to do is make your day about him."

"Okay, bitch I'll drink to that! Girl! Here comes Ray."

"Excuse me, ladies, Reece, can I speak with you for a moment?"

"It depends on what you need to speak with me about."

"I will make it brief." I take a moment to think it over. "Okay, excuse me, ladies. Ray, what do you want to talk with me about? Are you about to tell me why you're fucking my sister and married to one of my closest friends? You being here even befouls me, and don't act like you don't know what the fuck I'm talking about."

"Whatever is going on in my personal life is not your damn business. Therefore, I will not further entertain you with this ignorant bullshit."

"Nigga, please! Yea, you'll entertain me as long as I say. Before I conveniently tell Mia, your wife, that your girlfriend is my sister, Ashleigh."

"I don't know what Ashleigh told you, but we're just friends. I asked to speak to you about the Roberson file."

"What you can do is send me an email when I'm back at the office. I will not discuss business at a celebration acknowledging my best friend. Bye, Nigga." I walked away, something he isn't used to most women doing to him.

"Hey, Babe! I didn't know you worked with my sister and Olivia."

"What are you doing here?" Ray asked.

"Don't greet me like that. What's your problem?"

"I'm here with my wife, and I didn't know Reece was your sister."

"What the hell does Reece, being my sister, have to do with you? I don't care about your wife being here. You don't call on your wife when you're eating my pussy."

"Reece has everything to do with this because she's best friends with my wife."

"First off, Olivia is my sister's best friend, and who is your wife?"

"Mia, Mia is my wife! I'm not trying to cause a scene in front of my colleagues, so I'll call you later."

"Nigga, don't dismiss me! I didn't know Mia was your wife, nor do I give a fuck. So don't call me later. Go keep playing happy husband in that sad-ass marriage."

CHAPTER 3

MIA & RAY

" Babe, would you like the family vacation to be in June or July this year? I thought we could take the boys to Riviera Maya in Mexico."

"Why are you asking me? Don't you plan our family vacations?"

"You don't have to be an ass, Anthony. This is not your courtroom! I'm only asking because I don't know if you have a trial or something else with work going on. I'm trying to avoid a scheduling conflict."

"I don't care what month you choose. You can see I'm listening to something. I just want you to stop talking."

"Being rude is unnecessary." Uggh, he makes me so angry! I don't understand why he speaks so rudely. "I'm going over to Reece's house." She always brings me back to a happy medium.

Reece must have seen me walking across the street. Before I could ring the doorbell, she was opening the door.

"Mia! I was just about to call and ask if you wanted to come over and patio sip with me."

"Yes, you read my mind."

"What's wrong?"

"I'll tell you but pour me a drink first," Mia said as Reece ushers her inside. "Girl, Anthony has been such a weirdo lately. I don't know what's going on with him. He isn't himself."

"Oh, really? Seems like his normal pompous asshole self to me."

"Reece! *She's right, but she doesn't have to say that.* "Please stop it. He's been under a lot of pressure trying to make his way into the political world."

"Mia! You stop always making excuses for Ray's bad behavior. We are all under pressure, and it does not give him a reason to treat you away."

"I sometimes wonder if he still wants to be married to me."

"You should be happy if he doesn't."

"Why would you say that?"

"Are you truly happy with him? I was hoping you wouldn't give me a rundown on how good he is with the boys. Instead, tell me how he is with you and why you want to continue to stay and deal with his abuse."

"He does not abuse me."

"Well, what the fuck do you call it? He never takes you anywhere unless it's with the kids. He intolerably speaks to you and treats you like you're his assistant, as if your only role is to complete chores for him. Duh, you're abused!"

"I stay with him because he's my best friend, the father of my boys, and the man I've loved since I was 16 years old."

"So – I can't believe what I'm hearing – it's justifiable because you've been with him since you were 16?"

"Makes what justifiable?"

This bitch! "His actions, Mia, his actions! How is he your best friend, and you don't even know what's happening with him and where he is half the time? If that's what a best friend and loving husband is, no wonder I don't have one."

"I'm not giving up on my marriage."

"I never asked you to. I asked were you happy, and you still have yet to answer the question. More wine?" I try to make light on the heaviness in the room. "We're going to LA for Livy's birthday. You should join us."

"When is it?"

"Next month, on the 18th, we will fly out on Thursday evening and return the following Monday."

"Let me make sure Ray doesn't have anything planned, and I will confirm later this week."

"Girl! I'll let you know how the trip was."

doorbell rings "Hey, bitches, y'all having a soirée without me? I came to pour the tea on the "D" I had last night annnnnnnnd this morning," CJ yells as she enters through the door. "Ooooooo, pour it! At least somebody is getting some dick in this circle."

"What bitch? You have a live-in dick. How is it possible not to be fucked regularly?"

"Mia, please don't say that out loud again, or I'm taking your pussy to be fucked by the biggest black dick I can find…Now! CJ, spill it!"

CJ scooted to the edge of her seat for dramatic effect. "When I tell you that young bull busted me down."

"The trainer boy from the gym?"

"Yes!"

"Bitch he's a toddler."

"His dick isn't. He fucked me so long, so strong, and so hard. I was begging for mercy or a sip of wine, whichever cum first, and I'm talking about my pussy."

"Oooooooo, I can't!"

"Shit, I can, and I did. I was sucking, slurping, and swallowing. Mia, honey, you want me to connect you with some dick?"

"No, I'm married!"

"So! Do you even like that nigga boy?"

"Yes, he's my husband."

"Girl, bye. Let me know when you are ready to stop fucking with that goofy ass husband of yours."

"CJ!"

"What? You were thinking it. You just didn't say it."

"Reece, what's going on with you and Eric?"

"Don't change the subject bitch."

"I don't want to talk about Eric," I said in a very dramatic tone. In hopes, CJ would stop asking about him.

"Why? What happened?"

"I'm too disappointed and embarrassed to talk about it."

"Is it that bad?"

"Yes!"

"Damn. Well, when you're ready to talk about it. I damn sure want to listen." *This bitch will not let me make it.*

"Oh no, Reece. I'm so sorry. I know how much you care about him."

"Yes, and I don't know why I continue to allow him to treat me like this...I'm lying. I know why."

"Ummmm, okay, why?"

"Because I hope one day, he will notice the value in me and choose me."

"Oh, Honey!" CJ didn't waste any time. "We're not going down this rabbit hole. You are too strong, too intelligent, too talented, too classy, too established, and too damn beautiful to pull out the worthless card. So have your pity party tonight, but tomorrow, pull your shit together, adjust your crown, and move the fuck on. Now, roll me a blunt. You've stressed me out."

"Okay, I'll roll to that!"

"Did y'all hear that Amber lost the baby?" CJ asked

"What? That's horrible. I'm scheduled for a hair appointment this week. Is she working?"

"I have an appointment this week too."

"What day?"

"Saturday, Liv and I both do."

"Mine is Friday evening. Do you know what happened?" Mia inquired.

"I can't give any details due to client privacy rights, but you know she'll tell you when you get your hair done."

"Really, CJ? That nigga probably stressing her out with his broke ass."

"I won't confirm nor deny."

"Well, why the hell would you partially pour the tea."

"I just wanted to make you ladies aware so that you can check on her."

"She didn't need to be pregnant by that bummy ass nigga anyway. He has her and some other

girl pregnant too. They are due like a month or two apart."

"Whaaaaat, Reece! How you know?"

"She told me."

"Reece, that was not your place to disclose that,"

"Bitch, you brought up the conversation. Hints that you wanted to talk about it, per usual, without being the one who poured the tea. FYI it still makes you messy bitch!"

CHAPTER 4

C.J.

Push! Push! Push! Harder! He's almost here. I see you crowning, PUUUUUUSH! Here he comes. Great job, mom. You have a healthy, handsome baby boy. The nurse will get you guys all cleaned up and get you to your room.

"Brandon, are there any more deliveries scheduled today? He responded, "no ma'am.""

"Good, clear my schedule for on-call the rest of the day. I have a few more errands to complete before the Razzle Dazzle this Sunday."

"How old are you turning, Dr. C?"

"Whatever age I want to be."

"You're such a smart ass. You have a phone call, Dr. C, It's Reece."

"Tell her I will connect with her when I get to my car, heading out now."

"Siiiiiiiiiiiiiis!"

"What's wrong, Reece? What's going on?"

"Eric! He's been really funny style lately. He was in town, we made plans, and he canceled on me last minute. He told me we would get together before he flew out, and he left without even a call. He claimed his flight got moved up. It's been almost a month. I hardly see him, and I'm always last on the agenda when he is in town. He was in town and didn't even think to prioritize me. He's short via text, and our messages are far and between. I feel like we're ending, but I don't know what I've done wrong for him to be so distant."

"I'll tell you where you went wrong. You're too damn available for him. Why are you waiting around on him anyway? What is he doing that has you that caught up? From what you described to me, it doesn't sound like much. Why haven't you snatched off the bandage and let that shit breathe and heal? Instead, you're nurturing a scabbed wound. Why are you begging for his attention when you have men lined up begging for yours?"

"He said we were good. Unfortunately, things have just been busy with work, and he's short on time."

"Oh, is that what he said? Did his work or career change?"

"No."

"I didn't think so. He had all the time in the world when he was trying to win you over. He had time to fly you in and out of the county or wherever he was at that moment. You're highly intuitive. Girl, stop playing stupid. Leave him right where he has you fucked up at. Yes, he is a catch but so are you. Yes, he has a successful career but so do you. You're 35, no kids, black and beautiful; Girl, fuck him! I'm heading to the bakery to drop off my cake topper and by Saks to grab a fresh pair of black Choos for my birthday soiree. Do you want to ride out?"

"I'm stuck inside today. The firm caught a big case, and all eyes and hands are on deck."

"Wait! You're calling me frantic behind a man. Meanwhile, the firm is working on a big case that needs your attention. I'm only going to say this once, Don't Lose Focus! He's not your husband. He's a guy you're dating. This career is what you've worked hard for and what's taking care of you. He hasn't lost his focus or priority, but you, my dear, are on your way. So don't lose focus!"

"You're right, sis. Thank you for bringing me back to reality. I'm going to let you get your errands handled, and I'm going to dive into my work. Let's get a drink later when you get home."

"Okay, boo. I'll talk to you later." Hmmmmmm, I may have a little time to pull up on my young bull. Let me call. "Hey, black man! What are you up to?"

"I was just about to text you. You were on my mind."

"Here you go with the bullshit that makes me wet... I mean smile."

"Yea, well, let's talk about it then."

"I like it better when you're tasting it instead of talking about it."

"Yea, FaceTime me that pussy."

"Or you can take time and put your face in my pussy."

"Pull up on me... Please."

"I thought you'd never ask. I love it when you're pleased about it. I'm sorry, I'm not trying to cut you off. Mia is chiming in on my other line. Let me take her call, and I'll see you within the hour." Hey Mia!

"Chole, are you busy? I called the office. They said you were out."

"Yes, I needed to do some last-minute things before Sunday's party. What's Up?"

"Two things. One, will you get the boys this evening? Anthony has a fundraiser meeting tonight, and I have to be present for it. Two, I made an appointment for this Friday with you. I'm having some issues with my strawberry."

"Yes, I will get the boys, but what do you mean issues?"

"The last couple of times, Ray and I tried to be intimate, and I couldn't get wet. He seemed very frustrated with me."

"Mia, there is absolutely nothing wrong with you or your strawberry. He is your problem. You aren't even forty yet. You're not going into menopause. You just had a pap, and your estrogen levels were normal. The cause for your dryness is mental. Your strawberry won't produce any juice because it's turned off. Your body is not attracted to a man who lies to you, cheats on you, belittles you, shows you no affection, has sex with you at his leisure, and you want her to drip juice for that same man. It doesn't work like that."

"What should I do?"

"I'm not sure that's a question for me. It would be best if you guys saw a therapist or a divorce attorney."

"I would never take the boys from their dad."

"Is that what you heard me say? Divorce doesn't mean he loses his kids. It means he loses access to you, and boundaries are established. You will know what to do at the right time. Meanwhile, you should also see a therapist for your mental health."

"I'm so confused and don't know what to do. I don't want to break up my family."

"You didn't break up your family... he did. You're not confused. You're hurt. You're in love with a man who does not love you back. I want you to stop holding on to the history of this relationship and start focusing on its strength."

"I'm going to call you back. I need to lay down for a minute."

"Mia, you are my friend, sister, sweetest treasure and sounding board. I'm here when you need me. You're going to be okay. I got you and the boys forever."

"I know, and I love you. Oh, don't forget the boys must be picked up before 5 pm."

"Okay, I'll call and check in a little later."

"Okay, talk to you then." Siri! Play Meg Thee Stallion. Plan B!

CHAPTER 5

OLIVIA

"What do you think we should?"

"Liv, I understand your reservations. We've only been dating a couple of months shy of a year. But I love you and truly want to spend the rest of my life loving you and making you happy. However, at the end of the day, I don't have a say-so over what you decide to do with your body. I support you."

"I just made partner at the firm. Ryan is almost five, and I don't want to be a 2nd-time baby momma. But, I desire to share that excitement with my husband this time around."

"You're not a baby momma. You're a single woman who's independently raising her daughter. I wouldn't leave you to raise another child on your own. I want to marry you, but you said you're not ready."

"Patrick, are you listening to me! I JUST made a partner; I'm still building a name for myself. The stakes just went up ten times higher for me. I'm a woman, and I'm black in a predominantly male environment. I don't have time to take a leave of absence to nurse a new baby. I want to marry you too, but we're both still building our careers. A baby and marriage would alter our plans tremendously."

"Okay," Patrick says with a hint of defeat in his voice.

"That's all you're going to say is, okay?"

"What do you want me to say? You got it all figured out."

"Ryan, come on. Let's go now."

"So, you're walking out in the middle of a conversation?"

"You ended it for me."

"Okay," Patrick says again.

As soon as I made it out of the door, I quickly went to the group chat. SISTERS! Code Red!

Report here. I need a girl's night NOW. 7 pm???

Reece: I'm in. What are we celebrating?

CJ: Yeeeeeeeeeeees

Mia: Count me in

Ava: Why tonight? I have some pre-scheduled pussy plans.

Olivia: I'll say it, and we can discuss it later.

CJ: Say what, girl?

Ava: ????

Ava: This better be important if I'm missing pussy on my face tonight.

Reece: Liv, spill it already!

Olivia: I'm pregnant

Reece: LMAO Bitch stop playing. I'm with Ava. I don't have time for this fooler today.

CJ: Hahahahahahahahaha Yea Right.

Mia: Livy, that is nothing to joke about. Now that you have our attention. Let's hear it.

Ava: This is so childish.

Olivia: Seriously, guys! Do you think I group messaged you for an emergency meet-up to lie? ABOUT A BABY! Patrick and I just got into it because I want to terminate the pregnancy. Reece: WHAT BITCH! Why wouldn't you tell me we were best friends.

CJ: WHAT

Mia: WHAT

Ava: WHAT

Olivia: Are y'all coming over?

CJ: Of course!

Ava: Yes

Mia: Yes, my love

Reece: Whatever

"Ryan, you will stay the night at Gigi's."

"Why?"

"Your aunties are coming over for ladies' night."

"Can I come?"

"Not tonight. We will have a girl's night tomorrow. I promise."

"Okay."

"You're such a big girl. You're my dream come true." I finally made it to my mom's house. "Mom, we're here. I'm rushing out because I need to skip traffic." My mom calls for Ryan to come up. "I'll see you later; mommy's big girl."

This better be as important as Liv claims. This is the last night Eric is home, and she wants to call a damn code red. Why the fuck is she not on birth control? The Bitch knows it's the 21st century, and there is such thing as Plan B. Since she wants to be irresponsible and not use a condom. These bitches better not say one word about me being late either, or I'm walking right out. "Hey, hey! Sorry, I'm late. I got caught in a little traffic."

"You didn't miss anything. I just started telling them the story. Can y'all believe I'm

considering having an abortion? Why is this happening now? You should have seen the look on

Patrick's face when I mentioned having an abortion. It was the look of disgust, and he was

lying, saying he supports me."

"Hold on. You can't say he was lying. You don't know what he was thinking or feeling. Patrick

is a good guy. If he says he supports you, he does."

"CJ," Reece interjects. "This is not the time for you to give analytical support. I mean,

seriously."

"Girl, back the fuck off. I'm speaking with reasoning. You nor her, as I said, don't know what

he was thinking."

"CJ and Reece, let's not fight about this. We have to figure out a plan."

"What plan? I'm not okay with abortions," CJ says. "Why weren't you protecting yourself if

you knew you weren't on birth control? Patrick is a great guy. What's so bad about having his

baby?"

"Did you really just say that, CJ? First off, I just made a partner. I have been trying to become a senior counsel for the last five years of my career. I'm 37, unmarried, and I have a 4-year-old daughter who is about to turn five that I'm currently raising alone. You all do know that. I still have student loan debt and other significant obligations."

"All I heard was you saying me, me, me. Have you considered how he feels? When he has

clearly expressed his love for you openly, he adores Ryan. You knew you had all these

obligations when you were letting him raw dog your ass. You are more than equipped to have another child. Count this baby as a blessing and keep moving forward."

"Are we about to encourage her to keep a 2nd child when she's clearly expressing that she doesn't want to? I'm about to pour myself another drink, smoke my blunt, and pretend CJ didn't just say none of the bullshit she just said. Also, Mia, honey, this really isn't a conversation you should join in on."

"What is that supposed to mean, Reece? You've been pretty funny acting over this last week towards me. Is there a problem?"

"When there is, I'll let you know first."

"REECE, you should take a walk. I understand you're upset, but what we're not going to do is attack one another while one of us is already down," Ava interjects.

"I'm sorry, guys. This is my mess, and I will clean it up."

"Girl, hush! We would never let you go through this alone."

"Right, I don't think you should abort the baby, and an adoption is always an option. Whatever you decide, I'm rocking with you."

"We've been through much worst. We will get through this too. Somebody check on that crazy ass Reece!"

"I'm going since her beef is really with me for not telling her first about the pregnancy.

CHAPTER 6

AVA

I love it here. I love being by the water. It's peaceful and calm. It almost feels as if the water is music-making love to your soul. The wind gently blows the trees, and the beautiful, colorful flowers are blossoming. This is bliss!

"Yes, it is. How did you find this place, Ava?"

"I'm drawn to water. I have been for as long as I can remember. My mom used to take me swimming a lot. She loved the water too."

"How long has it been since you lost your mom?"

"It's been three years, and it still feels like three days ago."

"I understand your grief. I can't imagine your pain. You carry it so well."

"I don't have a choice. I'm all I have."

"That's not true. What about the ladies you hang out with? I hear you call them sister a lot."

"Yea, you're right. They are my family. I mean, I have no other blood-living family I know of. It was me, my mom, and my grandmother when I was growing up. I lost my grandmother seven years ago, and my mom followed."

"That's tough, but don't forget that you are so loved. Blood only makes you related, not family."

"From what you told me, you have an amazing family."

"Yea, I do."

"I need to head back so I can get ready for CJ's party tonight."

"Yes, I remember you saying that was tonight."

"Mel, what you got up for tonight? Would you like to come and hang out with us?"

"Yes, I would. Thank you for asking."

"Cool. Can we meet at my crib and leave from there?"

"Yes, that works."

"Come through around eight or 8:30 pm."

Oh, shit! They lit up in here. Ayyyyyyyyye! On my momma, on my hood, I look fly and good. Ayyyyyyye, turn me up, Reece!

"Who is that?"

"That's Melissa. She goes by Mel."

"Who is Melissa? I don't know her. Where is Brandi?"

"Could you leave me alone, girl? I love pussy, and pussy loves me."

"Uggggh, you're such a little whore."

"I know! Ayyyyyye"

"Ooooooo, Ava, you are looking good bitch! I like that side fade you added to your hair. So who is that girl you're with?"

"That's what I asked the whore."

"Mind your business and stop asking so many questions you don't want the answer to," Ava respond while smiling.

"Where is Brandi? We like her."

"I like her too, but she's not here tonight. Mel is. Deal with it!"

"Reece, I thought you were mad at Eric, yet you still showed up with him to my party."

"Right! She's always the kettle calling the pot black."

"Fuck Yall! We made up."

"Okay, for how long," Ava asked.

"You are a real hater."

"Nah, I just recognize when a nigga is full of shit."

"I'm done. I'm going to get Eric a drink."

"Yea, you do that!"

"Hey man, what's up!" Eric responds, "Ray! My boy, how have you been?"

"Ava, look!"

"Look at what?"

"Ray and Eric are over there talking."

Ava quickly turned her head to see what is going on. "What the hell? I didn't even know they knew each other."

"There goes Mia. Call her over here."

"Mia, what the hell are Ray and Eric over there talking about."

"Girl, I don't know. Leave him over there. We met Eric one night when we bumped into him and Reece at Monarch. They invited us to join them for dinner. He seemed nice."

"Girl, please! You're so angelic you don't recognize Satan himself when he's right in front of your eyes."

"Now, CJ, you're going too far."

"I'm serious! It's something about him I just don't like, on top of how he's been treating Reece lately."

"Yea, he really has been on some bullshit," Ava agrees.

"So, Eric," Ray asks, "how are things in the Real Estate world? The median sales price has risen almost 25% since last year."

"Actually, man, it's a sellers' market right now, and the housing sector is solid."

"Shid, it doesn't appear that way."

"Are you guys in the market to purchase a new home?"

"No, noooooo. Mia loves that house. She's the reason we built our home in that community. This year will make five years of us living there, and the goal is to make it another five years. Not to mention the 750K ticket it cost me to live there."

"Yea, man, I get it. Hopefully, I'll purchase my dream home soon."

"Wait, you don't own a home?"

"I own several homes, but not my dream retirement home. I travel and work too much to be able to enjoy it."

"Maybe you and Reece can build that together?"

"Oh, she'll definitely like that."

"What are you men up to? You guys have been over in this corner for about an hour." "Mia, you look stunning. How are you?"

"Thank You, Eric. I'm doing well, as I hope that you are."

"I'm well, and it's good to see you again. Where did Reece run off to?"

"She went to get me a drink and never came back."

"You know her; she's a natural social butterfly. Anthony, my love, can I steal you away for a moment?"

CHAPTER 7

REECE

"Bae, where did you go? I thought you went to get me a drink?"

"Oh, I'm sorry, babe. I got distracted talking to Ms. Brenda. I hadn't seen her since she retired from the firm. I got you an old fashion on the rocks, coming right up."

"Don't get distracted this time, please. I'm already feeling out of place from the sideways look your girls are giving me." Yea, I'm sure they are. Trust I've told them about some of your questionable acts. "Stop It! They aren't looking at you any kind of way."

"Shid! The girl who's hosting the party didn't even speak."

"Pay CJ no mind. That's just her personality. She has to warm up to you. She's the momma bear of the group. Very protective!"

"Yea, whatever."

"Hey Reece, come on. Let's go out back and take a smoke intermission," Ava says while approaching me. "Hell, Yes. Give me a second; let me take Eric back his drink and see if he needs anything else."

"Damn, he can't get his own drink?"

"What the hell is wrong with all y'all today?"

"Girl, just hurry up. I don't want to leave Mel left alone for long. She doesn't know anyone here."

"Neither does Eric."

"Hell, he was just chopping it up with Ray for a while."

"They don't know each other like that. We recently had dinner with him and Mia not too long ago."

"Who knows? Maybe they were having a clown reunion. Just hurry!"

"I'm coming. Start rolling us up, and I'll be there."

"Reece! Where are you running off to?" *If one more motherfucker stops me. I'm going to scream!* "Outback with Ava. Join us?"

"What the fuck took you so long," Ava yells while lighting up.

"Bitch, didn't I tell you I had to give Eric his drink? He started talking, then I bumped into Livy, and now we're here. So shut the fuck up and lite me up."

"I know, Ava! She gets on my nerves, too. What are you doing here with Eric, anyway? I thought you stopped fucking with him." *These bitches are always bringing up old shit. That happened last week. We are in the present.* "Ummm, why are you bitches so pressed about Eric and me?"

"BIH, you tried it. I'm never pressed about no dick. I eat pussy. You told us you were done with him, and here you are tonight with him."

"Exactly, Ava! Livy chimes in, "don't pop yo shit with us, then turn around and call us about that nigga later."

"Fuck both of you Anime-looking bitches. I appreciate your concerns, but we're good now. We have decided to make things work. Yes, he was on some bullshit. But, he has apologized and promised to do better. That's all I can ask for, right?"

"Tuh! You shouldn't have to "make" things work. The definition of make is to cause something to exist. You shouldn't be causing a relationship to exist. That should be organic."

"Your heart, not mine."

"Why are you so freaking weak behind Eric? Don't bother giving me a lecture on my relationship as long as you're accepting his bullshit."

"Touche, sis!" Let me change the subject because these bitches don't know when to leave enough alone.

"Liv, what did you decide to do about the baby?"

"I don't know... I don't know."

"Well, you don't have much time to procrastinate."

"I Know. I'm confusing myself. I don't want to hurt Patrick, and I don't want to postpone my career either."

"I'm unsure if either of us can advise because neither of us has had a baby. Just know whatever I can do for you and my little sweet pea Ryan, I will."

"Girl, she knows we have her back."

"It's just a friendly reminder bitch. A friendly reminder!"

"I probably shouldn't be getting high with you heffas till I decide to Boss Up & Ball Out or Carry & Marry."

"This is not the time for jokes, bitch! We better get back inside for Madam CJ comes out here and regulate our asses."

"Where the hell were you hoes?" Sure enough, CJ was right there, ready to interrogate us. "Outside, captain hook. Relax."

"Don't tell me to relax. You walked off and left me with Ronald McDonald and Bozo the clown."

"Girl, I just said the same thing. Them niggas went to the same clown university. Dressed up circus acts!"

"Chill the fuck out with the clown banter. Okay, I get it, you bitches not fucking with Eric."

"Shit, you shouldn't be."

"Well, I am. Let's move on."

"Yes, because Eric nor Ray are not worth my energy or ruining my mood at my party."

"Who is that guy with trainer bae?"

"I thought that too. He has big dick energy."

"Oooooh, girl! That's Elijah, and he absolutely has big dick energy. He's the General Manager over those gyms Ross trains at."

"Calm down, pregnant Patty."

"Girl, hush! I know how to look without touching."

"What's going on over there with Mia and Ray? They look like they are getting into an argument?"

"Oh no, not tonight, not at my birthday celebration!" "Excuse me!" CJ says with an attitude while talking to Mia and Ray. "What's going on over here? You two are causing a scene."

"Don't worry. We were just leaving."

"No. Ray, I'm not leaving. I'm enjoying my best friend's birthday party. You can go."

"You're leaving when the fuck I say you're leaving."

"Hold On! She said she was not leaving. Walk yo ass right out the door you walked through, or I will have you escorted out, and it won't be polite."

"See Chloe! Mind your own motherfucking business."

"If I don't, I can guarantee you can't make me."

"I got it, sis! But, Ray, I'm not ready to leave yet. I will see myself home when I am."

"Bring your motherfucking ass on right now! Before I cause an even bigger scene."

"ROSS!!! Will you and the security team escort Mr. Lastra the fuck off my property before I have him arrested?"

"Bitch fuck you! I'm leaving!"

"Raymond! Why would you talk to CJ like that? That's so unacceptable and inappropriate. She's the boy's godmother."

"Since you're so worried about Chloe, you are right. You should stay the fuck here."

"Reece, what's going on over here," Eric asks with a concerned look on his face.

"Hold on, babe. This hoe ass nigga is disrespecting my friends."

"This is not your business. Stay out of their shit."

"Whatever THEY are involved in is MY business. I see you're on some bullshit too."

"I'm about to go."

"BYE, Nigga! See ya. Wouldn't want to be ya!"

"You see, Reece. I told you that nigga was goofy!"

"I don't know why he's acting like that tonight."

"I'm over the whole fucking night," CJ says. "I'm minutes from asking everyone to leave."

"No, no, no. We are not ending the night like this."

"Let's get some drinks and turn the fuck up! One time for the birthday, bitch. Ayyyyyyyyyyye!"

CHAPTER 8

OLIVIA

“Yo babe, what was that! Shit got real tight in there real quick.”

“I know. Ray is always mishandling Mia. We don't understand why she stays with him. She is literally one of the most brilliant intellectual speakers I've ever heard. Her research on how the brain function and operates is fascinating. Mia was on track to become a profound therapist.”

“That shit is crazy how he was talking aggressively like that to her. I thought the dude Reece was with was coming over to deescalate the situation. Instead, he goes over and amps the shit up.”

“Eric is a whole other story. He's been playing pity pat with Reece's heart for over a year. She's so in love with him she overlooks every sign that's presented to her.”

“Has Ray ever hit Mia?”

“Um, not really... hit... that I know of.”

“What the hell does that even mean?”

"She told us he grabbed her and pushed her down once. She hasn't said anything like that again since that one time."

"What! She doesn't have any brothers or a father present?"

"Mia isn't from here. She moved here with Ray after they graduated from college years ago. He is the only family she has here, outside of us. The girls!"

"I don't care if my daughter or sister lived on another planet. I'll go wherever she is and be on that nigga's ass."

"Maybe she hasn't told her family. Living a happy life via social media and a plane ride away is easy. She can pretend to be happy with them, but it's different with us because we see and talk to each other damn near every day. Rarely do we go longer than that."

"You just stay out of his way. The story will be told differently if he ever handles you in any way."

"Okay, baby. I wouldn't want you to go to jail behind me. I'm about to call and check on Reece before we go to bed."

"Giiiiiiiirl! Are you sleeping?" I couldn't dial Reece's number fast enough.

"I'm so glad you called me. I didn't want to call you because I knew you were with Pat."

"What the cluster fuck was tonight?"

"I know, right? I'm so embarrassed for Mia and me. That is Ray's normal behavior, but Eric, I can't believe it!

Sis, I'm so hurt. I've been calling and calling him. He won't even answer his phone."

"Why in the hell are you calling him? He's the one who needs to be calling you. He disrespected you in front of your friends and walked out on you. You are tripping."

You know what, Liv is right. He tried to handle me as if I had done something to him. That's the reverse psychology narcissist shit I don't like. But, in the same breath, I wonder if he still wants me. OMG, I am tripping. "Do you think he's met someone else or just lost interest in me?"

"Bitch, if you don't pull yourself together. This is not the Reece I know, tucking her tail and running behind a man. I am not dismissing your feelings. They are valid. But why are you allowing a man that barely makes time to see you a priority in your life?"

"I know. You're right. I feel so defeated and unwanted."

"Reece, it's okay not to be okay. You just can't stay here. I will not tell you to pray because you may be too weak. Instead, I will pray for you that God mends your heart and gives you the strength and courage to move forward in the will he has ordained over your life. This chapter with Eric may end in your life, but remember, a new, better one will start. God never takes something from you to hurt you. Instead, he prepares you for what's next. Find the lesson and learn from it."

"Thanks, best friend. I have no words left. I just need to lie down and try to sleep this feeling away."

"I understand. I love you. Send a smoke signal when you need me. Goodnight."

CHAPTER 9

C.J

"Good Morning Dr. C! We really enjoyed ourselves at the party. Thank you again for inviting my husband and me."

"I'm so glad you two enjoyed yourself, despite the misunderstanding towards the end of the night. I apologize."

"No, apologies are necessary, but I couldn't figure out why Reece was there with Mr. Washington."

"Who? She was there with her boyfriend, Eric."

"Oh. Excuse me for not minding my business."

"No, you're good. What's up?"

"You don't recognize him? He's been here in the office a few times. His wife or girlfriend is pregnant. She sees Dr. Okoye. I'm pretty sure I saw him here with her on her last visit. He was holding her hand and carrying her purse."

I could not believe what I was hearing. "WHAT! Are you sure? Is Dr. Okoye here today?"

"Yes, he is with a patient."

"Will you let him know I would like to speak with him when he is available?"

"Sure thing. Dr. C, please don't tell Reece. I would hate to see her beautiful face sad."

"I would never mention your name in any conversation regarding this matter. You have my word. She is one of my best friends. I have to let her know if she's being played. But I will fact-check before I relay and information. Thank You, and we never had this conversation."

"Yes, ma'am, and I'll get Dr. Okoye for you."

Siri call Olivia. "Hello LIV! I have something urgent and very sensitive to tell you. What time do you get off work today?"

"I have a few minutes to talk. What's up?"

"This is not a conversation for on the phone. I know you will see Ava if she isn't already in your office. Tell her code red and to meet us at our spot at 7 pm."

"Okay, but what is so urgent? Can I know that?"

"It's about Reece."

"What about Mia?"

"What about Mia? I'm not calling to tell her shit. Did you know after Ray humiliated her like that in front of everyone, she still left with him?"

"CHLOE JACKSON! Stop it! Mia is your best friend and part of this sister circle."

"Well, if you want her to know so badly, call and tell her."

"And I will. Bye. With your rude ass," Livy stated.

"BYE!"

Let me text Ava and Mia. Hey Ladies! CJ has called a code red for tonight. Please meet us at 7 pm at our spot. Let me know if you will be late or can't make it. She said it was vital and didn't give many details over the phone.

Mia: Yes, I will be there. I wonder what's going on? I haven't talked to her since the party. We were supposed to go to brunch the next day, but she sent a text canceling. I hope everything is okay.

Olivia: She's okay. She said it's about Reece.

Ava: Yes. I can make it, and I'm always down for tequila and tacos. Lol Reece isn't coming?

Olivia: I don't think so. She said just us.

Mia: Okay. I'll be there. See you guys later.

Ava: Whatever! Liv, do you want to walk over to Starbucks with me?

Olivia: Girl, yes! I need a double shot of espresso. I'm coming out now.

"Hey! So, what's going on with Reece," Ava asked.

"I'm not sure. I know she was upset about Eric leaving her at that party in front of everyone."

"Nah, I think she is okay with that now. I talked to her last night, and Eric was over there. Plus, she just told me to bring her the pink drink back. She only drinks that when she's in a good mood and she's putting on pink lipstick."

"Well, I don't know, and now I want to know what's going on?"

"What if she's pregnant? It makes sense. How would CJ know before us?"

"Hell Nah, Ava! That bitch is too superficial. She would be somewhere crying, chanting her life was over. We would have to admit her to an insane asylum."

"Yea, you're right. I guess we'll hear about it tonight. I think I messed things up with Brandi." "Why? I love Brandi. Did she find out about the other girl?"

"Kind of, sorta!"

"What in the hell does that mean?"

"You know I love being free and doing my thing. Brandi is just so reserved, and sometimes I feel bored with her."

"You do know you're in a relationship with her, right? Brandi is so good for you and to you. I know you have an upbeat personality while she's calmer, but think about how much balance Brandi brings to your life."

"I hear you, and it still equals boring or not completely satisfied. Don't get me wrong, I love Brandi, and the sex is fire. I just hate that sometimes she is closed off. She didn't come to CJ's party because she said, 'she didn't want to be out too late.'"

"Oh."

"See, I told you."

"Tell her gently how you feel and that you enjoy spending time in her world. Now you want her to experience yours."

"If only it were that easy."

"Right! It sounded good tho. Ugh, back to work we go."

"It's only three more hours. I'll see you tonight."

"Okay, bye, sis!"

CHAPTER 10

MIA & RAY

"Anthony! I'm getting ready to head out to meet the girls. Can you get Brenden? He won't let me leave." Brenden. Daddy is calling; go see what he wants. "Call him again, Anthony!"

"Come on, buddy. Mommy is going to go talk about daddy with her friends."

"Cut it out. I'll be back in a couple of hours. See you gentlemen later."

"Look who finally showed up."

"Hey, Ladies! So sorry I'm running a little late. Brenden was being a big baby tonight. He didn't want to stay with Ray. So, I had to sneak out when he wasn't looking."

"Even his 2-year-old son doesn't want to stay with him. So you're back calling him "Anthony"? Guess you aren't mad at him anymore."

"CJ, don't start! We are here to see what's going on with Reece."

"Okay, since we're all here now, I can tell you what I found out today from a reliable and confidential source. Eric is expecting his first baby with a woman name Sydney. Before all of you say it's not true, I could be fired because she's not my patient and patient confidentiality laws, but I looked at her chart, anyway. She listed Eric Washington as the father of her unborn child. He has also been to our clinic on several occasions with her. That's why I remembered his face, but I couldn't figure out how and where I knew it from. When he was at my party, I got a weird vibe from him, and didn't know why. I think it's because he remembered me from the clinic."

"Excuse, ma'am! Can you bring us another round of margaritas and add an extra shot? It's about to be an interesting night."

"Liv, you took the words right out of my mouth. We probably should have talked about this at one of your cribs because I need to smoke. What you just told us put me on edge," Ava said. "This breaks my heart for her. She loves him."

"Fuck Him! He doesn't love or give a damn about my sis with his trifling ass. I found her Facebook page. Check this shit out. He is literally living two separate lives."

"BITCH! Look at this goofy tight pants wearing ass fool and his hoe with that tilted wig on." "No. Don't attack her. She's a victim too. Should we tell her too?"

"Hell no, Mia! That bitch isn't our friend nor our concern."

"Exactly! Why she's over there making all these posts about him? He hasn't posted one thing about her on his page. He appears to be single."

"Who's going to tell Reece?"

"You are CJ. You found out first and told us this information. Plus, I don't want her cussing me out because she's definitely going to cuss you out about him."

"I would like to be there when you tell her."

"I think we should all be there," CJ replied.

"Oh no. She's going to feel attacked and like we plotted this because – truly– none of us has ever liked him."

"I agree with Mia. We should all be there regardless of how she reacts. She would be the first one there for any of us."

"Like three months ago, Ray and I got into a fight. Physical. CJ was on call at the hospital. I was terrified and didn't know what else to do. I grabbed the boys and ran down the street to her house. She comforted me. She wanted to call the police, but didn't because I asked her not to out of respect for me and the boys.

"Mia, what happened? Why didn't you tell us?"

"I knew you all would be upset and probably put a hit out on him or something. Plus, I knew, like always, I wasn't ready to leave him. The next morning, the boys and I went home."

"Mia, how can you live like that? You can't be happy," Olivia asked frantically.

"Some days are better than others. I have you guys and my boys. That's enough to keep me going. I may know precisely how Reece is going to feel. Ray also has an illegitimate child that's 10. He pays child support and has given up all his rights to that child."

"Sis, what the fuck! I never want to tell you what to do with your life, but you have to get out of that marriage. I don't think that's how it should be, and I'm not married. If that's what everyone is signing up for, I don't need it or want it. No wonder I like pussy.

"Now you see why I hate his guts. I've been friends with Mia for over ten years, and I remember when he got that girl pregnant. I told you then not to marry him. He asked to marry you to keep you from leaving him. He wasn't ready then, and to this day, he's still not prepared to be a husband to you. You deserve so much more; I can't make you see that. You have to decide on your own."

"I know. It makes me sad. I'm aware of how I'm being treated. I pray that God touches his heart before it's too late for us. I believe he loves me the best way he knows how. I knew going in he had mommy and abandonment issues."

"Why do you always make excuses for his disgusting behavior?"

"Because I love him. He is the father of my children and my husband. I'm sorry that you don't understand that., but I vowed before God and will endure a little more for God's promise to me."

"Don't use God as a cop-out. I hate when people do that. God never told you to be a fool. God never told you to stay with a man committing adultery on you. God never told you to stay with a man that's mentally and physically abusing you. Stop making excuses for him. You will leave when you've had enough, and I will be here to have your back."

"Mia, please know that we all love you, and we're here rain, sleet, or snow for you and the boys. No matter the time of day, we got you."

"Thank you."

"I think we should get our check so we can head over to Reece's house. It's almost 9 pm. Has anyone talked to her?"

"Yes, she's home."

"Okay, I got the check. Let's go."

CHAPTER 11

REECE

Long sigh as the tears flowed heavier and closer together. I slide down in a tub full of steaming water while eating a classic vanilla Nothing Bundt cake with vanilla bean ice cream from Crumbl, just constantly thinking. *Why is this happening to me now? What have I done so severely that this hurt is my karma? Lord, take this pain away. PLEASE!*

How did I miss him having a whole other life without me in it? Did he even love me? He was never planning on buying me that ranch and land. Why did he lie? I wonder what about her that's more special than me? I know she's not flyer than me or has a bigger bag. Why her and not me? I know she's not fucking him better than me. The way he moans, begs and then passes out immediately after. There's no way she loves him better than me. He screams when I barely suck the head – was that fake too?

All the epic moments we shared while creating memories can't be fake. No one can fake that, can they? Did he lose his attraction to me? *I changed my hair often.* But he said he loved my fly. That can't be it.

Lord, what did I do wrong? Why didn't he communicate his unhappiness with me? I'm mean damn; I'm not a basic ass girl. I'm dope as fuck. I'm intelligent, funny, and creative. I own my home; I have no baby daddies or drama. I have a six-figure career. I'm fine, fit, and I cook. Not to mention, I look better than most of these hoes on my worst day. *Wait, why am I trying to convince myself about my resume and qualifications for a job with no benefits?*

What the fuck am I doing? He is the one who has been lying the whole fucking time, not me. No wonder he kept talking about how much he loved kids. He knew he and his wife-to-be were expecting a baby. I'm so damn stupid. I can't believe this shit. *Please, Lord, allow me to go to sleep and wake up from a terrible dream.* This can't be my life right now.

Who is calling me back to back? Go away. Are you fucking kidding me? There is no way this scum bucket, trash can ass nigga is calling and texting me. The audacity of him to text, "Reece, I'm sorry. I never meant for this to get back to you like this. Please pick up. I just want to explain. At least let me apologize. I'm miserable without you. I kept her a secret because I knew I wanted this life with you. We can fix this. I want you. I love you." My only response to his countless missed calls and overwhelming text messages is; BOY, FUCK YOU!

Maybe I should shower and eat. I've been wallowing in self-pity and funk for two days. I just can't get up. I need another day

Fuck my life. Now, who is this? Olivia! Again? "ReeRee, why haven't you answered all day? What are you doing?" *Crying! What else do people do when they're betrayed?* "I'm sorry, sis." "I'm not trying to make it worst. I just want to check in on you. Have you eaten anything?"

"No, I'm not hungry."

"That's okay. I'm going to door dash you some food, and you can eat it when you feel up to it. I'm also having Patrick leave a self-care package at your front door."

"Thank You. I'm sorry for being snappy. It just hurts so bad. I just wish it would all go away. I miss him and wants to respond every time he texts."

"Reece! Why haven't you blocked him? Of course, he is going to text and call you. Stop torturing yourself and let him go. He means you absolutely no good."

"I know. I just want to know why?"

"There is no reason why outside of selfishness. Sis, I know this is hard, but he is getting married to her."

"What are you talking about, and how would you know that?"

"I searched on social media for her and found her page."

"What? Why didn't you tell me? How does she look? Is she prettier than me? What does she do for a living? What's her name so I can find her?"

"Reece baby, I don't think you want to see her page. It's photos of them on vacation, him celebrating her birthday, and their proposal. Let him go on! They're even building a home in the Farmhouse estates. She posts everything on her Facebook page. It almost seems intentional, like she is trying to prove he's her man. One thing I know for sure. God has better in store for you."

"I don't want anyone else. I want him. He promised me a life he's giving her."

"Hold on. Ava is beeping in; I'll merge the call. Hey Ava, I have Reece on my other line. I'm about to merge you in.

"That's who I was calling you to check on. She's not answering me."

"She just told me to conference you in. Reece. Ava.?"

"Yea, I'm here."

"Ava! I just want to go far, far away."

"No, babe. What are we going to do without you?"

"I'm so hurt that I can't even think of anything else but him and what I could have done so wrong."

"You've done nothing wrong. He was too weak and not strong enough to love you."

"My sentiments exactly, Ava," Olivia agreed. "I told her that. Right now, ReeRee, your faith in God sounds really small. Don't you believe God will send you a man better and more deserving of you than Eric? So, what you're saying is you want to go back to a man who has an unspoken baby on the way by a woman who has magically appeared in the picture? Time-stamped pictures showed approximately three months ago. He asked to marry her around the same time he started tripping, acting funny, and disappearing on you? He has lied to you repeatedly and has disappointed you over and over. So, that's the man you want to run back to?"

"Well, not when you put it like that. I really thought I met the one this time. I'm not getting any younger, and I want a family of my own. We've been together for 16 months, and I never saw this coming. I planned what I thought would be the rest of my life with an imposter. He took me ring shopping with no intentions of marrying me. What a slap in the face! He proposed to another woman... I feel sick."

"I know you do. I feel sick hearing this shit. Don't worry about it, I got your back. I have an idea."

"And what the fuck would that be?"

"We can remove his license plates off his car and flatten his tires!"

"Ummm, Jazmine Sullivan, calm down. We're not doing that.' But you know what? That shit would be funny as hell and may make me feel a little better."

"Nah, you both tripping! Girl, fuck him!"

CHAPTER 12

OLIVIA

"Hey Baby! How is your day going?"

"It's cool."

"What's up? Why do you sound like that? Sad."

"I made the appointment for the abortion today. It's set for next week. I was calling to give you the information and instructions that were provided for the day of the procedure."

"Are you sure you want to go through with this?"

"No, Pat. I'm not, but I'm now ten weeks pregnant and can't wait any longer. I don't want to wait too late."

"If you have to rush your decision and you're still unsure, maybe you shouldn't do it."

"It's not that I'm unsure of what to do. I just hate the choice that I have to make because of my actions. I'm sad because I will never get to meet this little face living inside me. It's just not the right time. That's the only thing I wish I could change is the timing. I want to have your baby. I just don't want to now."

"I don't want to do this, Olivia, but I will never let you go through something like this alone. I got you, baby. It will be okay."

"I know you got me, and I love you for that. But, heads up, Reece will be here when you get home. She's stopping by for a drink or two."

"Okay, cool. I'll stop and grab some food."

"Perfect, Babe. I'll see you when you get here. I got to go. Reece is ringing the doorbell like a maniac."

"Why the hell are you ringing the doorbell that many times?"

"Bitch! Move out of my way. I have to pee!"

"Oh, sorry, come in."

"Hey, Ryan, Auntie's favourite little person in the whole wide world. What are you working on in here?"

"I'm painting a picture for Aunt Ava's art show. She said I could."

"Yay, I'm so proud of you. Can I see? Ooooh, Ryan, that's so beautiful. I love it."

"Thank You, Auntie Reece!"

"I'm going to let you finish painting your art and go chat with your mom. Then, I'll come back and see you before I leave."

"Bitch! I hope you made my drink double the trouble. My mental health is holding on for dear life."

"Reece, stop being dramatic."

"I'm so serious. Do you know Eric is still going through with this marriage shit? She posted 60 more days till I become Mrs. Washington."

"Why are you looking at her page? I told you to block both of them."

"I know I can't help it, but he got me fucked up. So I'm attending that wedding so he can look me in my face when he says I do to her."

"What the hell, Reece? You are tripping. I'm not letting you attend this fool's wedding. They will have you kicked out of there in front of everyone. How many more times do you want him to embarrass you?"

"You can't let me do anything. I'm grown. Which is why you and the girls are coming with me to crash his shit."

"Oh, no, the hell I'm not. Sis, I got enough shit brewing in my life right now. You are letting him get the best of you. You are so much bigger than this."

"Hey Baby! What's up Reece!? What y'all got going on in here," Pat asks.

"Reece's ass talking about she's going to pull up at Eric's wedding."

"Aww shit man, Reece is trying to start a war."

"Patrick, that shit is not funny, and don't urge her on."

"Girl, shut the fuck up. Pat is not urging me on to do anything. Fuck Eric and that wedding."

"I'm sick of these weak-ass men playing with me. He's the one still calling and asking to see me."

"How, sis, if you blocked him like you said you were?"

"I unblocked him. Now what?"

"All shit to the side, he's playing you. I'm telling you as a friend and from a big brother's point of view. This may sound harsh, and I'm not trying to hurt your feelings. But, he's keeping you around for a rainy day."

"I appreciate y'all little intervention, but I'm good."

"This is the last thing I'm going to say and leave it alone because you're right, you are a grown woman. Reece, he didn't choose you because he didn't want you. He chose her because she is perfect for his image and career. Your strong take-charge personality is too much for him and the forefront of his career. Some men view that as aggressive and can feel you don't need him. He needs a soft, mild-mannered woman. A polite, pretty face, not a dominant beauty queen. You'll attract too much attention in his spotlight. I'm sorry; that's the hard truth. Listen to your girls and let him go."

"So, you're saying I have to dumb myself down, be quiet and be a yes girl? All for a nigga's ego? I can't help; I'm a boss, and I'm very unapologetic about it. I've worked too hard to become the Reece I am today to be sitting on the sideline mute. I refuse to be controlled and allow a man's ego to manipulate me. I don't need a man. I am the most real man I know in bad bitch

form."

"Yea. I hear what you're saying," Patrick replied. "If you know that, then why are you still chasing behind him? You keep saying you don't need a man because you have NEVER been with one."

"Chasing? I'm not chasing shit. He's the one saying he still wants me."

"Actually, he's just checking your temperature. He's making sure he can have you on reserve." "Sis, I think this nigga is trying to make you his side bitch."

"Exactly! He's definitely trying to keep her on the sideline. It's like an accomplishment. I have the prize and the runner-up."

"You got me fucked up! I'm not any runner-up, second best, or option to nobody, let alone another bitch. You've made your point Pat. I need to let it go. All of it."

"Sis, I know this is hard for you. Just take this time for yourself. You've had a rough couple of months. Maybe we can go on a girls' trip for a change in scenery?"

"You know what, that's not a bad idea. Minus the girls. I think I want to take a few days away alone."

"Are you sure? You know we will come with you. Where are you going to go?" I know, but you're right. I need some time to myself. Get your laptop, and let's book me a mini escape.

CHAPTER 13

AVA

❝ Yes, sir. I'll be there around 6:00 pm. I would like to look over the entire exhibit one last time before the guest arrive. I want to ensure the art is in place and hung according to the layout I submitted."

"Of course, Ms James. I assure you we're prepared to accommodate tonight's guest for your art exhibit."

"Thank you again. I will see you shortly."

"See you soon Ms James."

"Hey Ava! Is Reece here today?"

"Yea. I just left her office right before I caught this call."

"How is she today? Is she in a better mood?"

"I mean, she seemed okay. I guess, given the fact Eric had his baby this past weekend. She said she would be at my show tonight, so she is good. Liv, why are you asking me and not walking into her office and checking on her yourself?"

"Girl, hush and just tell me. I'm going to check on her. I wanted to know what mood she was in first."

"Bye Liv. I have to go. I need to finish getting prepared for tonight."

"Yea, yea, that's right. I'll see you later tonight."

(Knock, Knock) "It's me, Reece. Can I come in?"

"Really, Liv!"

"Heffa, I'm just asking. I wasn't sure if you wanted to be bothered or not."

"Why? I'm good. CJ told me that Eric's baby came early. Good for them."

"Good for them? Bye bitch, you're trying to be funny. Reece, please burn that bridge so that you never cross it again. I'll bring the gas and the matches to the party."

"Seriously Liv!"

"What? I'm just saying they don't call me the "Pope" for no reason."

"Oh, cause bitch this will definitely be a "Scandal.""

"What time does your flight leave on Sunday?"

"It leaves at 7 pm. I'm counting down these last couple of days till Sunday."

"I can't believe you're not letting your best friends come with you to Puerto Rico. We'll be there for moral support."

"Trying to guilt me won't work. You know I'm selfish."

"You suck!"

"I know, and I don't care. What are you wearing tonight to Ava's art show?"

"I'm trying to figure that out. I don't know if I'll have enough time to go home and change. I have to pick Ryan up from my mom's house, and Patrick is coming to the show straight from work. That doesn't leave me too many options."

"Why can't you just leave here early? I'm leaving at 4 pm sharp. As a matter of fact, let me set my out-of-office email now for today and next week."

"Uggggh, you really do suck!"

"And Bay-Be, I'm going to look bomb 1st in this hot pink Roberta Einer dress tonight. I'm outside, biiiiiiitch!"

"Bye, I'm going back to work. I'll see you tonight."

"Hey, ladies! What did I miss?"

"Hi CJ! We all just arrived about 10 mins ago. The show hasn't started yet. I like those shoes, honey."

"Oh good, I thought I was late. Thank you, Mia. Where are the boys?"

"There with Ray's brother and his children. He took them to see a movie."

"I will not bother asking where Ray is... because I don't give a damn."

"CJ, why are you so ill-mannered?"

"Shhhh, Ava is going on stage."

I want to take this time to thank God and all of you for coming out tonight and joining me in my first art exhibition. I'm excited and humbled to invite you into the mind of Ava James. I titled this exhibit "Dark Spaces" because we all have found ourselves in that space a time or two. A space of uncertainty and desperately looking for a light at the end of the tunnel. I want to thank my mom and my sisters (Reece, Olivia, Mia and Chloë). Your continued love and support have given me the confidence to believe I can accomplish whatever my heart desires, and I

work hard for it. I want to thank my girl, Brandi, for keeping me focused, grounded, and never complaining about the nights I didn't make it to bed when I was up all-night sculpting, drawing or painting. I love and appreciate each of you. Kings and Queens, thank you again for coming to celebrate with me. Now grab yourselves a drink and enjoy the show.

"Awww Ava! I'm so proud of you, and you look so beautiful."

"Yes, you look gorgeous. I love the entire art collection. I'm taking home the "Born and raised a Black Woman" painting. It has a strong ancestry vibe."

"I love that one too! Thank you, guys, for helping make my dreams come true."

"Girl, we didn't make your dream come true. You did that on your own. We just had the pleasure of watching and cheering you on from the sidelines."

"Let's go take some pictures before the 360 booth gets too crowded."

"I need to go fix my lip stick first."

"Come on. We don't have time for that. You see all these people waiting to talk with Ava."

"Shut up Liv! I don't give a damn about these people waiting. I'm not taking no picture with no crusty lips."

"Right. How does mine look?"

"You both look perfect. Now seriously, come on."

We finished taking our pictures in the 360 booth. "That was so fun! Let's go get another drink." "Liv! Look at me. Don't panic because no one is looking."

"What!!! What are you talking about?"

"Look down; you have blood running down your leg."

"What the hell! Oh No!"

"Stop, don't make a scene. Start walking towards the restroom. I need you to lock the door so no one comes in and sit up on the counter, so I can check you. Are you feeling any pain?"

"No, not really. I'm slightly cramping, but I've been cramping on and off for a couple of days." "Why haven't you said anything?"

"It wasn't bad or lasting pain, and this is my normal time of the month. So I thought since I wasn't bleeding, I was fine."

"Liv, baby, you're having a miscarriage."

"No, I'm not. I can't be having a miscarriage. I haven't done any abnormal activities, and I'm not stressed about anything as far as I know."

"Girl, are you fucking kidding me? Ever since you learned about the baby, you've been on edge."

"Reece, we don't have time to talk about this right now. We have to get her to the hospital." "Should I call an ambulance?"

"NO! Reece, you go get Patrick, tell him what's going on, and to follow us to the hospital. Mia, you go quietly and tell Ava what's happening. You stay with her till the end of the show. MIA! Did you hear me?"

"Yes. I'm going."

"Fix your face first. We don't want to draw any unnecessary attention. Liv, can you stand and walk? "

"Yes, I can make it to the car."

"Listen Mel; you knew I had a girl."

"No, you told me you were broken up."

"No, I told you we were taking a break."

"It didn't sound like that when you were giving your speech."

"Ava! I need to speak to you for a moment," Mia interrupts.

"That's rude. You didn't see me talking to her?"

"Excuse me, I apologize. Ava, it's important. May I speak with you privately?"

"Look bitch, I was trying to be cool, but I will cause a scene in the middle of my art show. Don't ever fucking talk to Mia like that again or we gone be knocking all this shit over. You can leave anyway. I invited you as a friend, but since you can't respect that I got a girl or my sister, you can get the fuck out." I turned to walk away and talk to Mia. "What's going on Mia?"

"Olivia started bleeding, and we're not sure what caused it. Chloe thinks she may be having a miscarriage."

"A miscarriage? Where is she?"

"Chloe drove her to the hospital. Patrick and Reece went with them."

"Let's go!"

"No, I'm going to stay here with you till after the show."

"I'm not staying here!"

"Yes, you have to; this is your first show. You have waited for this time to shine for too many years to leave in the middle of it. Olivia is okay. The show is over in two hours, and there is nothing we can do at the hospital but wait. If anything changes, I'm positive that Reece will call and let us know. Let's get a shot and calm down. You got this!"

"I really want to be there with Liv."

"You will in two hours."

CHAPTER 14

C.J

" Patrick. Liv wants to see you."

"Is she okay?"

"Mentally and emotionally, no. Physically, she's going to be okay. She will need lots of rest and to stay off her feet for a couple of days, but she will recover just fine. Unfortunately, Liv has had what we call an inevitable miscarriage. Due to the bleeding, cramping, and her cervix being dilated, we consider a miscarriage to be inevitable in happening. I'm so sorry Patrick."

"Thank you, C.J! I appreciate you being here to help us through this."

"Reece, will you call Mia and Ava to let them know where we are so they can come over? I can't remember where I put my phone."

"Yes, I texted them already."

"Liv is going to need all of us. She's now very remorseful and emotional about her original decision to have an abortion. She feels like this would have never happened if she never planted that seed. I told her this wasn't her fault. It was going to happen either way because of her cervix dilating."

"My heart is broken for her. I didn't really think she wanted to have an abortion. I just thought it was the idea of having two kids and not being married yet. Plus, the pressure of being a female attorney in a predominately male workspace. Can I go see her?"

"She asked to speak with Pat first. So, let's give them a moment and go grab a coffee. I think she needs his emotional support right now."

"I'm just so sad."

"Yea, me too."

"I need to call my sister to let her know what's going on with Liv."

"Oh, yes, I totally forgot to tell you to include Ashleigh. Of course, we all know how she loves Liv."

"Hey ya'll, what's up? How is Liv? Can we see her?"

"Patrick is in with her now. They still have a few more tests to run. She will stay overnight for observation, but she's going to be okay. Reece just stepped out to call her mom and sister to let them know what's going on."

"Where is Ryan?"

"Liv's mom took her on a walk."

"Good evening, everyone," Ray stated as he walked in.

"Ray," CJ mumbles.

"CJ," Ray responds.

"Hey Ray. What's up," Ava asks.

"Ava, congratulation on your show tonight. I apologize for my absence. I had a prior engagement I had to be present for."

"I understand you're a busy man. Mia bought a sculpture for you guys. I appreciate the support."

"Okay, cool. I can't wait to see and hear about the show."

"CJ! What is Ray doing here?"

"Girl, I'm sure Mia made his trifling ass come."

"Ashleigh is on her way."

"Okay, cool!"

"Ain't no okay, cool! Ashleigh and Ray are fucking around."

"What the fuck are you talking about, Reece?"

"I know. I think I fucked up."

"WHAT! Omg. Tell her not to come."

"I can't because she stopped and picked up my mom."

"What the fuck! Why didn't you tell me?"

"I didn't tell anyone, I was trying to keep Ash's slut activities private, and I didn't want to hurt Mia."

"I'm actually embarrassed."

"Why? That's her pussy, not yours."

"But why would Ashleigh fuck with Ray? Mia doesn't deserve that. It's 100 men after her, and she wants to fuck with a married one that's our friend's husband."

"She claimed she didn't know that Ray was Mia's husband. His goofy ass claimed he didn't know she was my sister."

"How is that even possible? We've hosted too many events that they both were present at to be pretending not to know one another. So if that's the lie, they both agree with, okay!"

"Exactly! That's why I checked his ass. He knows I'll never tell Mia this bullshit, smug bastard."

"You won't tell her, but I damn sure will."

"I'm coming back, Reece. I'm going to see if they have found a room for Liv so that we can visit with her."

"Hi Reece."

"Brandi, how are you? I didn't get to chat with you at the show. Everything happened so fast."

"I know. I'm doing well."

"I was trying to get over there to tell you how pretty you looked, per usual."

"Aww, Brandi, you're so sweet. Thank you! Did Ava sell out her showcase?"

"She did really well. She has a few pieces left. She is going to list them online for viewing and purchase."

"That's a great idea. We're so proud of her. Excuse me Brandi, I need to go speak with my sister for a minute. Ash, I'm telling you right now, be cool and don't start no shit in this hospital."

"Girl, hush. I'm not thinking about Ray and whatever he has going on."

"I'm serious. This is not the time nor the place. I would not have told you to come if I knew he was coming here."

"Reece, you are tripping. Olivia is family, and I was going to be here regardless if he was here or not."

"Whatever! I just tuned you out. I'm trying to hear what CJ is saying."

"Okay, everyone, they are moving Liv to the 7th floor, room 716. We're allowed three people at a time to visit, especially during this covid crisis. So I'm asking you to please visit briefly so that we may all have time to see her before visiting is closed down for the night. If you can't stay, we will release her in the morning, and you can call or visit her at home. (CJ waves for Reece to come over). You gone have to get Ashleigh out of here."

"WHY?"

"Mia just asked me if Ashleigh was in any kind of legal trouble. I said not that I know of. Why? She said that Ashleigh keeps talking down low with Ray, and when she asked him, he said Ashleigh needed legal counsel regarding a domestic violence case."

"CJ, please tell me you are lying? I specifically told her to stay away from Ray while at this hospital. Mia is no fool, she knows something is off, and she knows her husband. Where is she?"

"Outside with Ray... go get your damn sister."

As I'm running through the halls of the hospital hysterically looking for Ashleigh. I started thinking, why am I worried about Ashleigh's shit? This is her shit. Why does her shit keeps involving me? This is not my shit. There goes the bitch. "ASHLEIGH! Why in the hell do you insist on being a little hoe? This shit is tired and old. Grown women in 2022 get their bag and their own man. I'm not about to keep track of no young dumb 28-year hot pocket that doesn't have any money in her pocket. You fucking around with all these niggas with a check but ain't collecting any bags. I'm not talking about no mother fucking purses."

"I never asked you to keep track of me. I live my life for the moment, in the moment. Yea, I may not have "a bag", but I also don't have "a bill". Those niggas you are talking about pay my rent, utilities, car, hair, nails, shopping, partying, travelling. Should I go the fuck on? You worried about me when you should be worried about you, and why you let that lame square ass nigga dog you for a bitch that don't have "a bag". You and your boogie ass friends may have a bag, but none of you bitches have a man, including the married one.

"Oh, little sister, you have so much to learn. By the time you get my age, you'll be used up with no education, no resume, no experience, just a baby momma, on welfare and still borrowing money from me. Those are niggas you speak of because they're definitely not men. Men don't pay for pussy. They will soon be fucking with the younger, better version of you because you're not getting any younger, and they're on to spending with the next best hoe. Honey, you're not kept, you are controlled. You have to call and ask for money. I just go withdraw my money. Since you're popping yo shit, be sure to stand on that shit."

"So, you're choosing hoes, you barely know, over me... your sister? Fuck you Reece. You'll never have to worry about me again."

CHAPTER 15

REECE

" Hello, I'm checking in for Sharice Ryan."
"Good Afternoon Ms. Ryan. Welcome to The St. Regis Bahia Beach Resort. May I have your photo ID and the credit card you used to reserve your room?"

"Yes, of course. I reached to hand the tall, slender, soft-spoken young lady the items she requested from me. She blushed and said, "You are so pretty, Ms. Ryan." I responded, "oh, thank you, boo! You're so kind." She went on to compliment my off-the-shoulder white lace-trimmed, embroidered, floral maxi dress by Karen Miller. Accompanied by a pair of Tory Burch caramel corn sandals.

"Here is your ID, credit card, and room key. You will stay in bungalow 34. You will have 24-hour room service; breakfast starts at 7 am every morning. As you requested, we will set up your breakfast at the beachfront daily until checkout. The Wi-Fi login and password are listed next to the phone. In the drawer underneath the nightstand, you will find menus of restaurants near our resort and a tourist guide. Should you need anything, please call the concierge desk. We will be happy to assist you."

Shit! She's killing my high with all this talking and instructions. Sweetheart, just give me my room key. I have checked into countless hotels and spas.

"Ms. Ryan! Is there anything else I can do for you?"

"I apologize, dear. I have a million thoughts running through my head in a matter of seconds. I watch her laugh loudly as she covers her mouth. *Am I high, or is she? I'm funny, but definitely not that funny.* "Enjoy your stay, Ms. Ryan. My name is Sophie, and I'm here till 9 pm tonight should you need something. *Lord, I think this girl is flirting with me. That's*

it... I'm done. Let me get to my room.

Oh wow! The water is so blue and beautiful. Let me group FaceTime with the girls so they can see my view. This place is insane.

"Hey Reece! Oh, honey, I live for that dress. So I know your ass is not just getting there?"

"Livy! No, I stopped at the bar when I arrived at the hotel for a little drinky drink. How are you feeling? I know damn well you didn't go into the office today?"

"Nope. I'm milking this time off. I'm in no rush to get back to work."

"Hey, people!"

"Heeeey Ava. Mia, where is that damn CJ?"

"When I talked to her earlier, she was working."

"It's 7 pm your time. She is not working. Anyway, y'all look at this. Hold on, let me flip my camera around."

"OMG, Reece, it's gorgeous out there! Will those doors close? You can't sleep with them open like that."

"Mia, stop mommying me and focus. Yo! Y'all will not guess who I ran into at the airport. It tripped me out. We were on the same flight."

"Forget that flight. I can't believe you didn't take us with you. What do you want FaceTiming me? You didn't want me to go on your little trip. So why are you calling us now?"

"CJ, go to hell. What are you over there doing? Why you're ten minutes late to our conference call."

"Right!"

"Who was on the plane ride?"

"Kendall!"

"Who?"

"Kendall, that short guy who was the principal?"

"NO! Ya'll remember Kendall. He was the guy who was a pilot for American Airlines. He sent me flowers to the office for over a month straight. Then one day, he never returned my calls or text."

"Yea, I remember him. So, what about him?"

"When we were waiting to board the plane. He came over and started talking to me. He apologized first and asked if he could sit. Then, he said he didn't mean to ghost me and that he wasn't ready for where we were headed. Finally, he claimed we were moving pretty fast and that he got nervous. Followed by, can he take me out again?"

"You've got to be kidding me. Why were you even entertaining his weak ass? He didn't even have the decency to call or send you a text. He disappeared."

"Okay, I was like, boy fuck you. Moving fast, we went on 3 or 4 dates, and I never fucked you. That's what you call moving fast?"

"Girl blocked his ass."

"Oh, he's blocked! He said he has tried massaging me on Instagram."

"Block him there too."

"No. I let them all have front-row seats to watch the show."

"Wasn't he like ten years ago?"

"No bitch, if he was, we wouldn't even be talking about him!"

"Anything over ten years... IT... DOESN'T... COUNT. Like nigga, who are you again?" The sound of us collectively laughing on beat comforted me. Things have been chaotic for all of us lately. Plus, I was too afraid to admit I was a little nervous about being alone on this trip. I have never vacationed alone before today. I clearly didn't think this through, but I realized no matter how far I go, they are there for me. "I'm hanging up with you whores now. I need to shower. I'm taking myself to dinner tonight."

"Please be safe Reece, and don't turn off your location for any reason."

"Yes, okay, Mia! I gotcha. I will check in with y'all later. Bye."

"Bye."

"Hi, I'm dining for one. Is the bar open seating?"

"Si senorita. Justo por aquíri." I assumed he was saying right this way as he walked ahead, pointing in the bar's direction. I responded with two of the five Spanish words I know, "Gracias Señor." This place is so sexy. It has a live mariachi band playing, dim lighting, and burning candles, with the smell of savoury and authentic Mexican food. I was in the right place, for once in a long time. "Hi, what can I get you to drink?" *Finally, someone who speaks English outside the hotel's front desk receptionist.* "May I have a gin & tonic, please?"

"That's a classy drink. You're undeniably not from around here." The dark-haired, handsome Spanish man sitting next to me turns and says with his rich accent, "I can also tell she's classy by the fragrance she's wearing." I smirked and responded with sarcastic disbelief, "is that right? What else can you tell about me?"

"If you join me for dinner, I'll be happy to tell you more about what I see."

"I don't know your name?"

"My name is Juan David, and yours?"

"I'm Sharice, but the people who know me, call me Reece."

"A beautiful name for a beautiful woman."

"Thank You. Well, since you're already sitting here, you can "join me" for dinner."

"I like your sense of humour and your smile."

"Flattery will get you everywhere, but nowhere with me." *I am intrigued, though.*

"Is this your first time in San Juan, Puerto Rico?"

"Yes, it is."

"What brings you into town?"

"I'm on vacation."

"That's interesting. Most women don't like vacationing alone."

"Who said I was alone?"

"I apologize. I didn't mean to offend you. I noticed you weren't wearing a ring. You said it was your first time here, and you're dining alone. So I assumed you were visiting alone."

"You're very observant, I see. Now that's interesting." *Huh, not only is he sexy as fuck, he's distinguished and meticulous. Nice suit too!* Time passed, and before I knew it, the bartender asked to close out our tab. I enjoyed Juan's company. He was so easygoing, and made me feel comfortable enough to bare my soul. There is nothing better than talking to a stranger. You never have to see them again, and they don't know you to go tell your business. "Thank you, Juan David, for an exhilarating evening.

"It was a pleasure Ms. Sharice. I hope to see you again during your stay here." *Ummmm, Juan David better stops coming on to me before his clothes start coming off.* "Yes, I would like that. Here is my number; give me a call; goodnight."

"Goodnight."

CHAPTER 16

MIA & RAY

“Why are we still on this, Mia? That was a week ago. I’m sorry that you’re so insecure that you think I’m sleeping with every woman I hold a conversation with. But, I will tell you for the last time, Ashleigh wanted some legal advice regarding a case she’s been charged with.”

“Why doesn’t Reece know about this so call case? She said Ashleigh hasn’t said anything like that to her.”

“Well, Reece isn’t an attorney, and maybe they aren’t as close as she portrays them to be. I don’t know, Mia! Ask her your damn self.”

“Can’t you get in trouble for interfering with an active case that’s not assigned to you? Reece may not be an attorney, but she knows the law. She could have asked Olivia for legal counsel. She’s known Olivia almost her whole life, and she’s their family attorney. It makes no sense. In every corner I looked around, you two were cozied up and whispering. Looked friendlier than business to me.”

“Whatever. I’m done talking about this.”

"I'm not done talking about it, but I'm leaving to meet Ava for lunch. I'm already running late." "Who's picking up the boys? "

"You are! Goodbye."

"Mia Lastra! You were just about to brunch alone."

"I know. I'm so sorry, Ava. I'll treat in gratitude for my tardiness. I was fighting with Raymond Anthony per usual."

"Oh, you big mad. You called his full name. What did that fool do now?"

"I think he was trying to make a pass at Ashleigh. Three different times when we were at the hospital, supposedly checking on Liv, I saw him and her looking very comfortable with one another. I didn't even know he knew Ashleigh that well."

"Yea, I peeped that too. I was wondering what they were up to, or at least, what was she up to? Ash is somewhat slick. Maybe she was trying to get information on one of her boyfriends in jail or some shit. Did you ask him while we're over here making up our own story?"

"I asked him, and he was defensive instead of giving me a direct answer. He eventually claimed she needed information for herself on a domestic violence case. I know he's lying because I called Reece the next day. She had no clue what I was talking about."

"Reece would definitively know if Ash was in trouble."

"The other thing is, I'm pretty sure I saw Raymond hand her a black card or something. He has a black American Express card. It's the only card that I don't have access to. He claims it's his business card for work. That same night, I checked his wallet, and it wasn't in there. I know there could be many reasons, but it's usually there."

"How do you know this, and why are you checking his wallet?"

"Sometimes, I check his wallet for hidden condoms. He lies so much, and I want answers."

"Mia, I don't know what to say. You should probably have this conversation with the other girls. I have zero understanding for his bullshit. I'll kill him about you. I will chop his body into little pieces and bury them all over the city."

"AVA!"

"The fact that you're checking for condoms tells me you already know he's cheating. I would hate to think that he or Ash would do something like that to you. I'm sure it's not what we think it is."

"I hope so."

"We can run it past Liv since we're going to check in on her after brunch."

"Thanks for reminding me. She said to bring her some red velvet chicken n waffles and beignets."

"Damn, I thought she wasn't pregnant anymore."

"Ava, filter, please."

After brunch, we get in our cars and head to Liv's place. "Hey, Liv heads up; we're heading your way. Don't bring up Ray unless Mia does.

"Why not?"

"She and Ray had an argument earlier today, she seems pretty rattled by it, and you can sometimes go too far."

"Girl, fuck you. I only speak the truth, and I wouldn't be her real friend if I didn't tell her the truth."

"That's your opinion, not the truth. You're confusing the two, and girl, don't stir the pot today. Please!"

"There is way more than you are saying."

"I'll tell you later; we're pulling up."

"I'm so upset. I have to leave. I can't stay."

"Why? Calm down. What's going on?"

"The children's ministry at the church had a "Sunday Funday" for the kids in the community. I let the boys stay after church to take part in the festivities. I told Raymond that I was going to lunch with Ava and that he needed to pick up the boys. The church just called and said the boys were still there and asked when will expect us to pick them up. I cannot believe him."

"Why aren't we in the car? We need to go get them. Liv, what are you doing?"

"I'm going with y'all too."

"What the fuck is going on, Ava? You called, and said don't bring Ray up in any conversations. Then Mia shows up in tears, saying Ray left the boys unattended at the church. Those are negligent charges, and Ray of all people knows that."

"I really don't know what's going on. Seriously. Mia told me when we were at brunch that she thinks Ray is trying to holla at Ash."

"What the fuck. Nah, I doubt it. Why does she think that?"

"Mia had some valid points. I even saw them acting in a very flirtatious way."

"When?"

"The night of my art show and when we were all waiting to see you at the hospital." "Biiiiiiiiiiiiiiiiiitch! What the fuck!"

"I KNOW RIGHT! "

"Damn, we need to call Reece."

"No, let's call CJ. Reece isn't back until tomorrow. CJ is right across the street and can meet us there."

"Put her on speaker."

"Bitch, this is 2022. There is a thing called Bluetooth that connects to your car."

"Leave me the fuck alone. I'm freaking out."

"CJ, where are you?"

"Hello to you Ava."

"It's me too, Liv."

"What do y'all want?"

"Meet us at Mia's house. Ray left the boys at the church after Mia told him to pick them up. Mia has been calling and calling, but he won't answer. She saw on the camera that his car is parked in the yard."

"His got-damn car is outside. I'm going over there."

"No, wait for us. We're literally 3 mins away."

"Okay, I'm getting dressed."

"Has anyone called the police?"

"Let's go in. I'm not standing outside waiting to see what happens."

"I hear them arguing. I don't want to just walk in. I'm trying to respect their boundaries."

"Fuck some boundaries. He crossed those when he left the boys at that church. You stand out here; I'm going in."

"Stop talking at me and like I'm stupid, Raymond. Don't forget we went to law school together. I may not take my bar exam, but I'm still the savviest Ivy Leaguer you know or have ever met. I would have been a judge before you knew you wanted to be. You forgot that I encouraged you to become a district attorney, and I ran a successful campaign for you to be in the position you're in today. You must have memory loss. How I remember the story is I allowed you to knock me up, and I "made the decision" to become your wife and be a "stay-at-home" mom. Never play with me about my boys because I'll end it the same way I helped start your career."

"Oh, now you talking like them bitches?"

"Woah nigga! I've never interfered with you and Mia's relationship, but you got the right mutherfucking one when you included me in it. I'm the bridge you never want to cross."

"Ava, get the boys and take them for a walk. They don't need to hear or see this."

"Ray, you should probably leave so that you can calm down."

"I'm not going no fucking where. This is my house, my wife, and my kids."

"That's okay Liv. I'm leaving. Raymond, please don't be home when I get back."

"I just said, I'm not leaving my mutherfucking house. We need to talk about this."

"You didn't want to talk about it before, so don't bother now. If you don't leave, I will. I will take the boys, and we won't come back."

"Oh, so you're putting on a show for these bitches? Let's see if any of them are going to take care of you."

"Mia, call the police. I would recommend you get a restraining order if he doesn't comply. I'm positive a new black judge on the bench doesn't want his personal affairs getting out amongst his colleagues."

"Fuck all that shit Liv! I'm sick of his weak, disgusting ass nigga. You can try that roaring shit with Mia, but I know you, Zeke, the cowardly lion. Let me let you in on a secret hoe ass nigga, I'm licensed to carry a gun, and this will be a self-defensive charge. I will shoot you with a kill shot to the head and go eat dinner after like nothing happened. Leave bitch ass nigga, NOW!"

CHAPTER 17

REECE

I'll miss you, Puerto Rico, but Dallas, I'm back! Home sweet home. Damn, I'm barely off the plane, and my phone has 17 new voicemails and 44 text messages. Hell, most of the messages are from Liv. *What the hell is going on? Why isn't Liv answering her phone? Let me try her office phone.* "Hello, this is Olivia Bailey. How can I serve you today?"

"Bitch, get the fuck on. I go out of town for three days and come home to CJ pulling a gun on Ray? Did I read your text message wrong?"

"Biiiiiiiiiiiiiiiiitch! In three days, three years' worth of shit has happened. Where are you?"

"I'm sitting in my car at the airport. I'm heading home. What's up, and why aren't you telling me what's going on?"

"I can't catch you up now. Mr. Brennon just called a damn meeting, and there is no short version to the story. When I'm off work, I will stop by your house. Ava has to tell you the first half because I wasn't there to say what happened. BUT BITCH! The second half is a scene from a Tyler Perry movie."

"What in the entire fuck? Tell Ava to come over with you. Is she going to the meeting too?"

"Yes, she is."

"Damn!"

"I have to go now, but I'm pulling up when I leave here."

"Okay, I'll be at home."

I need a drink! I can't get home fast enough. If it's not a nigga stressing me out, it's these bitches. What was the purpose of me going on vacation if I was going to come right back to this shit? Fuck a drink. I need a blunt. Siri, call my momma. "Hey Momma! I'm back. How is everything?"

"I'm so glad you made it back safely. But, do you know those planes are not safe? You need to stay your butt off those planes."

"Momma, stop saying this every time I fly somewhere. Do you need anything before I head home? I'm going to be in for the night. I need to get unpacked and settled. I just wanted to make sure you're okay before I do."

"I'm fine. Your sister came by earlier and checked on me. Then, she took me to that fancy store y'all always go."

"Momma, I don't want to talk about your daughter. I'm glad you're doing okay. I just wanted to check in."

"You two better cut this mess out right got-dern now. You all are all each other got, and whatever happened, it's not enough to cause you two not to speak to one another. You girls have always been so close."

"Okay, I hear you, momma. Is that all? Can I go?"

"Don't talk that sass to me. You go when I say. Bye!"

Now my momma is mad at me because her daughter is a hoe. Okay, then. I'm sick of these people. "Calgon, take me away!" Just when it can't get any worse, Mia lets the boys play outside. Fuck my life. I'm about to be fake and lie to my closest friend because my sister is fucking her husband. I'm such a lousy friend today. First of all, she should have been left that cheating sack of shit for a husband. She knows he's some dressed-up trash, and I mean garbage. Ash ole trifling ass done drugged me into the middle of this shit, but my momma is mad at me?

"Hey Boo!"

"Reece!!!! I'm so glad you're home, sis. I need to talk to you." *Oh shit! Here we go.* I'll come over once I unpack."

"No, I'll come over there. I don't want Raymond listening." *Oh, she's with the shits today. She just called that nigga Raymond.* "Liv and Ava are stopping by later. Are you okay with that? Is it something that they can hear? If not, I'm off work tomorrow. So you can come over for breakfast." *Please say breakfast. Please.*

"Yes, of course, they can hear. They were present for most of it." *Damn, Man. I won't be able to tell Liv and*

Ava about Ray's cheating ass. "Okay, that's cool, sis. I'll see you later."

"Hey, Reece!" *What now bitch.* "Yes, boo?"

"Can you make that drink you call "The Lil Wayne"? I really need one."

"AB SO-FUCKING-LUTELY!"

"Thanks, sis! I love you." *Yep! It just got worse.*

I guess I'll make some tacos with the drinks since I'm being all ho-SPIT-able and shit. On this week's episode of Mia and Ray, Ray cheats again. Mia cries, says she is done, and returns home the next day just to do it all over again. Wash, rinse, and repeat!

Let me stop. I was just crying over a goof-troop ass nigga who's getting married to a bitch making $12.00 an hour, screaming she's a model at 33 on Instagram with no real publications behind her name and no other goals or aspirations outside of being Eric's wife. He pretends that he's so boujee, and claims only to eat fresh, wild-caught seafood, but he is fishing out bottom feeders. I'll remind my damn self, "Girl, FUCK him" and the rock that he crawled from under. Whew, chile, I digress!

"It's unlocked. Come In."

"It smells good in here. You must have known I was hungry."

"Girl, get in here. We don't have a lot of time before Mia gets here. Ava, lock that door. I don't want her to walk in."

"Reece, what's going on, and why the fuck are you being weird? You left the door unlocked for us, but not Mia? Why?"

"Ava, shut your technical ass up and sit down. Listen, I know who Ray is cheating with." "Whaaaaat, pour the tea ret now."

"Ash is fucking Ray."

"Biiiiiiiiiitch! Ash, your sister Ash?"

"I knew some shit was up with the two. Mia was right."

"They've been messing around for a few months. I told Ash to leave him alone when I found out, but y'all know that's like talking to a brick wall with her. I want to talk to Mia about it. I just can't bring myself to do it. Ashleigh is my sister, and I have to ride with her. I know this shit is foul as fuck, but I can't tell Mia."

"Oh, no, ma'am. Ashleigh needs her ass kicked. She is out of line and code for that. She's never coming around Patrick again."

"I told her slut ass that. She claimed she didn't know that Ray was Mia's husband. I know she is lying. She just didn't give a fuck. Also, I'm pretty sure that Ashleigh's new BMW, Ray got for her."

"What kind of magic pussy does Ash have? Damn!"

"Mia told me she saw him hand Ash his black American Express Card. This shit is really messed up. Mia wouldn't dare do that to anyone. She's one of the most honourable women I know. Reece, I do not want to be in your shoes."

"I don't want to be in my own shoes. So, what happened? Why did CJ pull a gun on Ray?" "Now, since I know this essential piece of information, this all falls back on Ashleigh. Mia is assuming Ray is only trying to holla at Ash. That's why she's so disgusted. She will be devastated when she finds out they're actually messing around."

"Mia and Ray have been into it all this time over Ashleigh? Bitch, pour me another one of those drinks."

"Girl, and she's here. Please open the door for her."

"This is your house. You let her in. You're the one keeping a secret from her."

"Fuck you, Liv!" I hurried to the door. "Hey Mia! Come on in. We've already started drinking." "You should have called me. I would have come over. Give me a double of whatever is in that glass."

"Mia, you barely drink. You tried it!"

"No, I need it. Did the girls bring you up to speed?"

"No. Ava was just getting ready to tell me."

"Well, since you here Mia, you can tell her. I'm still pretty shaken up about it all."

"Okay. You all know Raymond and I have been on the odds for a while now. All the lying and cheating are making me depressed. The night of Ava's art show was the last straw. He told me he had a work event and couldn't make the art exhibit. Of course, come to find out, that was a lie. He was at dinner with some woman. Victoria, his brother's wife, told me. She said the woman wore a black dress with some long fake hair. When he arrived at the hospital, I was infuriated with him. I lost it when I looked up and saw him talking to a woman, not knowing it was Ashleigh. I only saw her from behind. She had long hair and a black dress. Reece, that's what I wanted to talk to you about. I said some not-so-nice things to Ashleigh. I wanted to get her number so that I could apologize. I know she has nothing to do with me and Raymond's drama. I feel so bad for acting that way with her."

"Mia, you said some not-so-nice things? You can never. I'm positive whatever you said to Ashleigh, she deserved it. I will have a conversation with her tomorrow."

"No, it's okay. I don't want to involve you. Raymond is continuing with his story, saying that she is involved in a domestic violence case."

"My sister is not in any danger. If she, the question is, why is she going to him? I haven't heard one thing about a DV case. I can assure you I'll find out when I return to work."

"I asked him those exact words and still don't have an answer, which brings me to how things escalated between us. I thought I saw him give Ashleigh his black American Express Card. That night while he was asleep, I went through his wallet, and his black card was not there. Before you get upset, Reece, I'm not accusing Ashleigh of anything."

"Honestly, you probably should be accusing her. Ash has some ways you don't know about. You said you asked Ray, and he claims it was nothing; then I guess it was nothing. The real question is, why did CJ pull a gun on him?"

"Ahhhh, yea! The next morning, he woke up on a rant, and I was still upset by what Victoria had told me. I told him before I left I was having brunch with Ava. He asked who was picking up the boys? I politely replied, "he was." The next thing I knew, the church called, asking who was picking the boys up. That made me even madder because I knew he was home doing nothing. He had no reason not to pick them up. I didn't know how CJ even knew what was going on. I later found out that Liv and Ava had told her, and we all know she hates Raymond. When CJ walked into the house, Raymond yelled, cursed, and acted like a complete fool. Ava took the boys to play, and Liv kept asking Ray to leave. By that time, it was too late. CJ was pulling her gun out and pointing it at him."

CHAPTER 18

OLIVIA

"Hey, good morning. Are you still sleeping?"

"Good morning, no, I'm up. I couldn't sleep at all. I want to slap the hell out of Ash myself. I texted her silly ass last night and told her to pull up on me today, and she goes, 'you have time for me today? I thought you'd be with your little friend Mia."

"Yea, Reece beat her ass."

"If I could get away with it, I would. But, that would break my momma's heart to see us physically fighting. It's already killing her that we're barely speaking."

"Did she agree to come over?"

"We're meeting for lunch at the Henry."

"What time? Can I come?"

"You know what, Liv? That's not a bad idea. Yes, come!"

"What time? Do you think it will cause more tension that I'm there?"

"Come around 1 pm. Things can't get worse with me and her than they already are. I don't even want to be around her, but I have to bribe or beg her some kind of way to leave Ray alone before Mia figures out it's her."

"I just knew she figured it out when she said Ash had the same look as the alleged woman Ray was out to dinner with. So I know damn well Ash wasn't bold enough to come to the hospital with Ray from dinner?"

"Nah, she probably would have if she didn't have to pick up my mom."

"Reece, let me call you back. I just pulled up to drop Ryan off with her loser daddy. I'll see you at 1."

"LIV! Don't call Andre a loser in front of Ryan."

"Girl, I didn't. Her headphones are on. I made sure I started her a movie before we left. I didn't know what was about to be said between us. You know how we can get."

"Oh, okay. I'll see you in a bit."

I turned my attention to my daughter. "Ryan, let mommy hold your tablet, and you get your backpack. Hi Dre! Please ensure Ryan has eaten and had her bath by 8:30 pm, so she's asleep by 9 pm. She is cranky like most 4-year-olds when they don't get a good night's rest." "Olivia, every time you drop her off, you don't have to go over a checklist with me. I'm her dad. I got this."

"Apparently not. As you just mentioned, I have to remind you every time like you're a 4-year-old."

"Liv, go ahead and leave before you piss me off."

"I don't give a damn about you being pissed off. I only care about the well-being of Ryan Nychole. Bye, mommy's big girl. I love you. I will see you tomorrow after school."

"Byeeeee, I love you too, mommy."

No, she didn't rush me off to be with her loser daddy. She is as crazy as he is. My poor baby doesn't know. I picked a bummy ass nigga to be her father. Thank God for growth and maturing my picker. It was off balance for a moment. Anyway, I'll stop by the office and then meet Reece and Ash.

"Hey, Reece. I'm walking in. Where are you guys sitting?"

"We're seated on the patio."

"Okay, I see you; I'm walking over. Hey, ladies. Ash, you cute or whatever."

"Livy! Thank you. I'm so glad you're feeling better."

"Yes, much better, thank God. Have you girls ordered yet?"

"Only cocktails."

"Good, I didn't miss much."

"Reece called you here to be the mediator between us?"

"No, bitch, I didn't. I called her here to be your protection so I wouldn't knock your ass out." "Reece! Chill."

"I'm not worried about her."

"But you should be."

"Hi, I'm Tonya! I'm your server for today. What can I get you to drink?"

"Right on time. May I have a lemon drop martini, please?"

"Have you ladies decided on any appetizers?"

"No, not yet. We need a few more minutes with the menu."

"Reece, we have to have this conversation like adults. Since you called this meeting, you should start first."

"This is not mediation or negotiation. So, Liv stop with the courtroom commentary. Ashleigh, I asked you to come so that we could speak directly to one another without interruptions. I've asked you on several occasions to stop fucking with Ray. Mia knows Ray is cheating and is very close to finding out it's with you. Why can't you leave him alone? At this point, you're being spiteful because I know you don't want him."

"I don't give a damn about her finding out it's me. That's your friend, not mine. I didn't marry her. He did. I didn't make her no promises. He did. I didn't commit a vow before God. He did. Therefore, I don't owe her an explanation. He does! And I'm not going to get an ass-whooping about it. You've made it very clear who you're rocking with. So, go tell her who he's cheating with, and I bet she still doesn't do shit about it."

"Hold on, Reece. Let me ask Ashleigh this question. What pleasure are you getting out of hurting Mia? There are one hundred other men you could date, but you choose to sneak around with Ray, a married man? Now, knowing Mia is our friend, you continue to mess around with him and put Reece in an uncompromising position. She asked you to back off. Why haven't you? I agree with Reece. You don't want Ray. You date big-name athletes and other prestigious men. Why now somebody's husband? There is no future there. You're too bright to allow a man to keep you in the dark."

"I love how both of you keep saying I don't like or want him. How would you know? The only reason either of you is making a big deal about it is that Mia is your friend, and Reece is

trying to keep her perfect image. I'm not about to keep sitting here defending myself from you. Neither of you is my momma."

"I'm so glad you said that because I recorded this conversation to play for momma. As long as you're fucking Ray, you have nothing to talk to me about. Fucking other women's husbands is bottom bitch shit, and I will never associate with that.:

"That's cool! Don't play it for momma; play it for Mia! It's her husband, not momma's, and now that we cleared that up, you ladies have a good day."

"No, Ash sit back down. We cannot leave like this. You and Reece are not talking."

"I'm done, Liv. I love you, but I'm out. I have nothing left to say!"

"Liv, let her take her ass on."

"Dammit! This was not supposed to happen this way. So, Reece! What's next?"

"I have no choice but to figure out a way to tell Mia. I could ask CJ to tell her?"

"No. You tell Mia like you just said you would. She will appreciate hearing it from you."

"I don't know. I don't know the first thing to say. I've been avoiding her because I can barely look her in the face, yet alone tell her that Ray is cheating with my sister."

"I know, right. We will think of a way and the best time to tell Mia. Don't stress too much about it."

"Hey! You never told me how your Puerto Rico trip was?"

"Shit, I never had a chance. It seemed all of you had more action going here than I did there."

"Yeah, shit has been crazy lately for all of us. But i have to run back to the office. I'll call you later so we can figure this out."

"Okay, bye. I'll sit here a little longer and have another drink."

"I understand. We'll talk later."

CHAPTER 19

REECE

I need to talk to CJ. Where the hell is she? I've been calling her all morning. She is not working that hard. Bitch swear she's delivering babies faster than Nolan Ryan pitching a baseball. I can't believe I'm this stressed over some dick that's not mine. We wouldn't even be in this situation had Mia left Ray a long time ago. She's pissing me off, too. If you want to allow this nigga to keep treating you like you're the lining in his trash can, go right ahead; however, stop including everyone else. Now Ashleigh's is blowing up my phone. *You didn't want to talk when we went to lunch the other day. I don't want to talk today. Fuck you, Ash! Finally!* Before I could even say hello, CJ was yelling through the phone, "REECE! Where are you? Get home now. Hurry!"

"I can barely understand what you are saying. What's going on?"

"Mia put a tracker in Ray's car and shared his location with her phone without him knowing. She tracked him to Ashleigh's apartment."

"FUCK! That's why Ash is texting and calling me back-to-back. *Damn, I shouldn't have silenced Ash's calls and texts.* I warned her stupid ass to stop messing with Ray."

"Ava is with Mia. She said they were headed to Mia's house now. Ava has a video of Mia jumping on the hood of Ray's car with her heels on, kicking his windshield in, while he was trying to get away."

"What in the hell? How did Ava get the video?"

"She and Mia took the boys to the art festival today. While they were there, Mia saw Ray's location was nearby, and he was supposed to be across town somewhere else. When Mia got to Ray's location, he was standing outside with Ashleigh, and they were getting in a black BMW and about to leave. Ava said everything happened quickly, but she managed to record most of it. She also said Mia and Ashleigh tussled a bit before Ray broke them apart."

"All of this happened in front of the boys? You've got to be kidding me. I'm leaving the mall. I should be home in like 20 minutes."

"Yes, it did. Things have gotten out of hand. Reece, prepare yourself. Mia knows you knew Ray was cheating with Ashleigh. Ava said Mia told Ray she was tired of him embarrassing and making a fool out of her. Ray told Mia, 'while she was busy kissing your ass, you were making a fool of her because you've known about his affair with Ashleigh all along'." *I'm lost for words. I don't want to go home, and home is my safe place. How is this falling back on me when I'm not the person committing any of the acts.*

"CJ, I need to call Ashleigh. I'll talk to you when I make it home."

"Okay, I'll meet you there."

I quickly hung up the phone and called Ashleigh back. "Ashleigh! What is going on?

"I'm on my way to your house."

"Why? Why are you coming to my house?"

"I'm coming to beat Mia's ass. The Bitch tried to show out today and swung on me.

"You're fucking her husband. You deserve to be swung on. Don't come over. I'm trying to get home to see what's happening and resolve this."

"It's no resolving shit at this point. I'm down the street from your house. Nothing will keep me from beating her ass today. I don't give a fuck about Ray, but when you disrespect me... now we have a problem, and the bitch threatened to report my car as stolen. Oh yeah, she has me fucked up completely. See you in a few big sis."

This bitch just hung up in my face. I cannot get home fast enough. This girl is going to drag Mia. *I'm right on time!* Ray is the first person I see as I turn the corner into my community. *I should run him over with my car. CJ should have shot his dog ass!* "You see this big ass mess you caused nigga!"

"Reece, you better get out my face before I knock yo ass back across that street!"

"Do it hoe ass nigga! Please do it!" I'm all in Ray's face yelling and pushing him, hoping he hits me so I can blast his ass. I'm not CJ, and I will not miss my shot. Ashleigh pulls up, jumps out of her car, runs over, and pops Ray in the face. Ray grabs her. I started punching and kicking hard as I could. Mia and Ava arrive, and things turned into one big backyard brawl. Our neighbours started coming outside. The boys were screaming and crying. I don't know when CJ or Olivia arrived on the scene. Police were everywhere. BITCH! We just turned one of the highest valued communities in Dallas, Texas, into the projects. My neighbourhood looked like Kappa beach in 1998, chaotic and rachet! I can read my neighbours' facial expressions. It loudly says, "it's always the black people bringing the property value down." I can guarantee Ray wishes he never met Ashleigh. This is going to be a massive hit against his career. Good luck running for Attorney General now, asshole.

"Hi, officer. Yes, I'm Sharice Ryan."

"Ms. Ryan, may I speak with you regarding tonight's incident and your involvement?"

"Yes, officer. How can I help?"

"Judge Lastra claims that you and your sister were trespassing on his property and assaulted him."

"Is that what he said? I live across the street at 1234 Dewberry Ln. Judge Lastra and I are neighbours. I visit Mr. Lastra's home frequently. His wife and I are close friends. So I wasn't under the impression I was no longer welcomed at their home."

"Ms. Ryan, can you give me your description of what happened tonight?"

"I walked over to check on Mia, my friend. Mr. Lastra started yelling and using obscene language toward my sister and me. When Mr. Lastra began getting more aggressive, I was frightened and defended myself in the best way possible. I can't confirm nor deny any other things happening around me. I was distracted defending myself and my sister from Judge Lastra."

"Ms. Ryan, did Mrs. Lastra ask you to come over? You mentioned you were going to check on her."

"No. I've never needed an invitation before. I was checking on her because another mutual friend mentioned Mia was upset because of an earlier altercation between her and her husband, Judge Lastra."

"The mutual friend's name is?"

"I would rather not release that information to you at this time, officer."

"Don't leave just yet Ms. Ryan. I may have more questions after I speak with Mrs. Lastra and get her description of tonight's events."

"No problem, officer."

"Reece! What was he saying?"

He was questioning me about my involvement in this circus. This shit is going to get back to all of our jobs. We work in the legal industry. I cannot lose my job behind this bullshit. That wasn't my bullshit, to begin with. I'm a couple of years from 40, and I'm outside fighting in the streets like some type of hood rat. Moving forward, I don't care, nor do I want to know what's going on with Mia and Ray. We all know she is going to sweep this under the rug and continue being with him like none of this ever happened."

"I agree with you. It's just not the time to point fingers. We still have to be present and supportive of Mia. She is our friend, and your sister played a major role in this mess."

"So fucking what! The keyword is my "sister", not Reece. I don't understand how either of you feel I can control an adult woman and her decisions. Ray knew he was married when he involved himself with a very single woman. Once he knew Ash was my sister, he knowingly still involved himself with her and didn't give a damn about Mia being our friend or the consequences. You can go be supportive of Mia, Ava. Since you understand her feelings so well, mine doesn't matter, anyway. Have a goodnight, Ava."

CHAPTER 20

C.J

" Mia! Mia, honey, you have to eat. Are you hearing me? It's been two days, and you can't keep going like this. The boys are coming home this weekend, and you need your strength. Would you like me to make you some food or order something from Bubbles -N- Brunch?"

"No, CJ. Thank you, I'm not hungry. I know you have to get back to your life. I will be okay alone for a while."

"Girl! I'm not leaving you here like this. Ava is coming over when she gets off work, and I'm on call until further notice. We will help you get through this and figure out what's next."

"I'm exhausted mentally. I don't have the energy or the fight to think about anything. I've spent the last two decades trying to please a man who I won by default. I can't remember who I am or the things I enjoy in life. I've taken myself out of existence and replaced my entire life around Raymond and the boys. So, excuse me for not recognizing my name being called. I'm unsure if I remember who Mia is or if she exists. This time is different. He didn't care that Ashleigh was Reece's sister.

He didn't even care that Reece and I were friends. He wanted what he wanted and didn't care if the boys and I got hurt in return. I've always known Raymond was selfish. He's been this way since we were kids. His mother taught him confidence, but his confidence turned into arrogance and anger in her absence. I was once told Raymond married me because I'm the prettiest girl in the room and that when a man marries a pretty face, he will never give her respect as his equal. She's the trophy he showcases. He has the status and the girl every guy wants. Judge, pretty wife, and two handsome boys. The image is complete. I guess my dad wasn't lying when he said that to me on my wedding day."

"Your dad is a pompous jerk! Yes, Mia, you are breathtaking. You're breathtaking because of the beauty you hold within. It flows through your heavily melanated skin, angelic smile, calming voice, and spirit. Your radiance is so magnetic that we're all so drawn to you. I will not sit and listen to you tear yourself down. I despise Ray, but I will never say he doesn't love you and the boys. He's too selfish to see your value because he is worthless. Ray does all these unforgivable things, not realizing the pain he's causing you. He's trying to ease his pain. You're the collateral damage in his storm. That doesn't justify his actions; it's his job to protect you and your heart. I don't believe it's a personal attack on you and definitely not on the boys. He's just too empty for you to keep pouring into. You will never fill him up. He is full of holes that need to repair. His peers see him as a handsome and successful black man. Society sees him as another nigga that they will only allow to grow so far and intentionally hold him back. He sees himself as God only knows what. I said all of that to say it's not your job to fix and repair him like he's some kind of project. You've done your part, more than your part. He has to heal himself. You didn't break him. I've been here through every season, and you've never wavered. Pick yourself up and decide what's best for you first. So that you can be what you need to be for the boys, and only you can determine what's next."

"Thank you, CJ. I'm grateful that you are here."

"Now, we need to sort things out between you and Reece. She has been calling and calling. You will eventually have to talk to her."

"I have little to say to Reece. She should stay on her side of the street, and I will stay on mine. She sat in my face for months, pretending she didn't know who Ray was cheating with. I talked to Reece about this situation a few times, and she knew her sister was sleeping with my husband all along. I can take that from Raymond. That's who he is, but should I have to from someone I call a friend and sister?"

"Mia, you know Reece wouldn't do anything to hurt you intentionally. She was put in an uncompromising position and wasn't sure what direction to go. I'll give you a little space to think things through; however, if anyone is granted grace through all of this, it should be Reece. Sit and think about how you would have handled it. Ava is on her way over here. You go freshen up. It may make you feel better, and I'll order food and make us some drinks." (Doorbell rings) "Hey CJ!"

"Hi Reece. What are you doing here?"

"I came to talk to Mia. I know she's staying over here, Liv told me."

"I don't think Mia is ready to talk to you. But, you do remember your sister fighting her in front of her children, husband, and our neighbours?"

"Yes. That's why I'm here. First, I want to apologize to her."

"Today is not a good day, Reece. This isn't about you, and you can't make her talk because you're ready."

"You can let her in, CJ. I will listen to what she has to say. I don't want to talk, but I will hear her out."

"Come in. I think this is a bad idea. You two are not ready to have this conversation. Both of your emotions are still running high. If either of you starts a yelling match, Reece, you will have to leave."

"That's understandable. I didn't come here to fight. I'm here to apologize for not telling you Ashleigh was having an affair with Ray. I was trying to avoid hurting you. I never condone Ash's behaviour. I asked her repeatedly to stop sneaking around with him."

"When did you find out Raymond and Ashleigh were sleeping together?"

"I found out at the celebration the firm hosted for Liv."

"Reece, that was last year. So you've known for almost a year?"

"That was not almost a year. That was seven to eight months ago. So I don't know how long they were involved. I only know when I found out."

"Reece, you're one of the smartest women I know. If you wanted to tell me, you would have figured out a way. I understand Ashleigh is your sister, and this was a tough place for you to be in. There have been many occasions you could have told me without ruining your relationship with me or your sister. I don't know if saying something was the right thing, but not saying anything is definitely the most hurtful. I trusted you. I told you intimate details about my marriage, and you sat there knowing your sister was the other woman. That's the part I don't know how to forgive you for."

"I don't have a rebuttal. I don't have an excuse. I just have an apology. I hope you will forgive me one day, and this will be far behind us."

"I'm not sure if I can forgive you. I don't even want to talk to you again after today. You stood by and watched this happen. You know how you always tell people, "Bitch, I don't fuck with you" ... those are my sentiments exactly!"

"Hold on, Mia. Don't leave. Where are you going?"

"I'm going home, CJ."

"Home, Ray is there."

"I'm aware. At least I know I'm sleeping with the enemy, and I don't have to worry about him being dressed as a friend. Oh, and Reece, tell your sister she can have Raymond in peace. I am filing for divorce."

"Mia! Wait, don't leave. Reece, say something."

"What do you want me to say, CJ? What can I say? She's not lying' I let this happen."

CHAPTER 21

MIA & RAY

❝ Mia, baby, I wish you would talk to me. Tell me how to fix this. I swear I will never lie or cheat again."

"Sir, please leave me alone. I'm enjoying a glass of wine, minding my business, and I don't want to consume your negative energy. I've drunk enough empty calories in this lifetime."

"We have so much vested together, over 20 years of friendship and almost ten years married. Baby, you don't want to break up our family. Think about the boys."

"Is that a trick question? I love how I'm being called baby today. You haven't referred to me as her in years. Shouldn't those have been your thoughts while you were committing adultery? It's interesting to hear you say, what about the boys? You didn't think about Brendan or Bryant when you made the executive decision to cheat on their mother. You broke up our family. I didn't. You're using the term family loosely. Other days, I'm just the mother of your children and the woman who cleans up all the messes you make with no repercussions. The problem is you don't value your boys or me. But that's my fault. I forgot my worth and fell asleep on myself. If you appreciated, loved, and respected me, this wouldn't even be a topic of conversation. I want you out of this house by the end of the week."

"I'm not moving out of my home, Mia. This is my house. I bought it. My salary pays for all of this. You haven't put one dollar in our accounts. All you do is spend the money I earn with your girl trips, designer handbags, shoes, spa days, private dinners, and all kinds of bullshit. I've never once said a word about your obsessive spending habit."

"You don't want to talk about monetary value and what I contributed? You wouldn't be in this position if it weren't for me. I paid your way through law school. I helped you win cases as your unpaid personal paralegal. I typed your briefs. I prepared every single speech you ever spoke. I ran your campaign, styled, and created your image, all while being pregnant twice. I'm raising two boys physically on my own. Your presence and support have been and will remain financial for the boys and me. The least you can do is provide because you damn sure don't protect. What else can you say you contributed outside money? I didn't think so. You will leave this house peacefully and quietly. If you don't, I will burn your entire life down."

"If that's how you want to play it. I will leave. You will call me back. You can't afford this life or house on your own."

"Oh, Raymond! That's where you're wrong. I'm not as stupid as you would like to believe. On our wedding day, my dad gifted me a rainy fund of 750k. Those girl trips, private dinners, and spa days you spoke of were a ploy. I took that money and added it to my rainy-day fund. It's been sitting and collecting interest all these years. Guess what, Raymond? It's rainy, and I'm not requesting a separation. Instead, I'm filing for divorce."

"You Bitch! You've been planning to leave me."

"How quickly I went from "Baby to Bitch" you're so predictable."

"We will see who the joke falls on."

"It has already landed on you. Good night, Raymond. Enjoy the rest of your evening."

CHAPTER 22

❝ Brandi, you're the best thing that has ever happened to me. I can't imagine not waking up to you every morning. You're the cream of my coffee, the bubbles in my bath, and my night light in the dark. Will you move in with me and become my wife? Please say that you will spend the rest of your days with me in this place we call life.

"Yes. I will marry you. I can't wait to have your last name. Hold up. Are you playing with me, bitch?"

"No, babe. You're crazy. Put this ring on."

"I'm getting married, getting married... getting married! Ayyyyye! I need to call my mama, sister, brothers, friends, co-workers, and everybody. I'm getting married, getting married!"

"You call whoever you need to, babe. I'm heading out to meet Mia and Liv at the gym. I'll grab food on my way back."

"I thought you went for a run with Reece this morning?"

"I did, but Mia and Reece are still not talking, and I don't want Reece to feel left out since we're not working out as a group."

"How long are they going to carry on with this? Mia knows Reece was not trying to hurt her. If I was Reece, I wouldn't have said anything either. I was always told to mind the business that pays me. Why isn't Mia mad at you and the other girls you all knew, too?"

"Because we didn't know! Reece told Liv and me a couple of weeks ago while we were at her crib for drinks. Of course, Reece kept that shit a secret."

"That's odd because I heard CJ telling Reece they should have told Mia months ago, and she should not have found out like that."

"What the hell are you talking about, B? How did you hear that?"

"I was standing next to Reece when CJ walked over to her, and they started talking about the police questioning her and not telling Mia before that day."

"Them bitches! CJ and Reece are foul for not telling her. It's cool. Mia knows now. However, if she stays mad, Reece deserves it."

"I disagree, but enjoy your workout, baby."

...

"Hi Livvy and Ms. Ava!"

"Hey Mia. How are you feeling?"

"I'm okay right now. Check back later."

"Right. I know the feeling, up and down, round and a round rollercoaster. You got this, Sis!"

"I'm praying I do. I asked Raymond for a divorce last night."

"Say what, bitch?"

"Liv! Volume. People are listening. Shocking, I know. I can't do it anymore. I can't even stand to be in the same room with him or hear his voice."

"Good for you, Mia! I'm so proud of you. Does this mean you're retaining me as your attorney?"

"Who else would I retain other than the "POPE?"

"Damn, now I don't want to share my good news. Mia just trumped it with hers, but if you insist. I asked Brandi to marry me, and she said yes!"

"Married! What! WHY?"

"I'm happy for you, Ava. I'm so glad that you decided to settle down with Brandi. We like her!" "Liv, what do you mean, why?"

"Bitch, you were just complaining about how bored you are with her, and now you want to spend your life with her? That's confusing. Every chance you get, you run off playing in the water with some other bitches."

"Who asked you for all of that, Olivia? A simple congratulations would have sufficed. You, Reece, and CJ are always popping off. Somebody is going to beat y'all ass up one day. Keep playing. It's me; I'm gone be the somebody!"

"And you're in your feelings! So, yep, you'll be retaining me next."

"Fuck you, Liv!"

"You two are both nuts. Come on, let's turn this anger into burned calories."

"OMG, and now Mia is starting with the Jane Fonda routine."

"Is CJ back from Vegas?"

"Hell, we should be asking you. You're the one who lives across the street from her."

"OLIVIA! You're such a mean girl."

"Thank you, Ava. I wear that title with pride, but to answer your question, I picked her up from the airport this morning."

"She didn't ride home with the guy she went with?"

"Nope. She told me the dick wasn't slapping."

"Well, I guess it didn't happen. Why did she go all the way to Vegas to find that out? She should have test-driven that shit here first."

"Nah, buddy lives in Vegas. He flew in to accompany her back there."

"He did all of that with trash dick? That's why he pulled out all the stops. I don't understand why y'all keep giving these niggas pussy. Y'all not turned off by now? The insanity!"

"Mia, are you ready to enter the pissy dating pool?"

"That's so far away. By the time I date again, God will have sent a new set of men."

"Wishful thinking! What are you and Ray's plan for the boys and the house?"

"We haven't discussed the split of things. One minute he's cussing me out, and the next he wants to make things work between us."

"Don't let him intimidate you. Would you like to file a restraining order on him?"

"No, I don't think he will do anything, and I don't want him to lose his job."

"Mia, you need to stop looking out for Ray and focus on yourself. You cannot move on by staying entangled with him. It's the too much history, memories, and love there that will keep you bound, so don't go full throttle; back away slowly and keep going without stopping."

"My entire body aches when I think of starting over by myself with two young boys. I graduated, went to college, graduated college, got married, and instantly started a family. I've never been on my own. I see you all do it with such grace, but I'm not sure if I'm as brave or strong as you all."

"You don't have to be strong or brave right now. We will be your strength and help you fight this battle. You need time to break down all those walls you built so that you can remember who you are when you look in the mirror and see yourself."

"Thank you, Olivia. You're not as mean as they say."

"Fuck them!"

"Girl, fuck you. Let's get this work. I need to get home to my wife-to-be."

"Here comes the bullshit!"

CHAPTER 23

REECE

66 This feels worse than my breakup with Eric. I've literally tried everything to get Mia to talk to me. Now I see how men feel with all the antics of getting back in our good graces. Yes, she has a right to be upset with me, but how is she going to be this hard on me for trying to protect her feelings? This bitch has clearly forgotten my role, and countless times I've been there for her. Let's take a stroll down memory lane. I was there each time he brought her an STD home. Don't forget, Ray is the only man she has ever been with, so she didn't contract the shit on her own. He flew a whole other bitch across the country, but won't even take her to dinner without the boys being present. Oh, and how could I ever forget he physically assaulted her, and she ran to my house, scared for her life? This nigga been for the streets, and I have to pay the price for his mishaps? Man, fuck that and her! *Nah, Reece, calm down and come back to reality.* I'm deflecting. I'm wrong. Mia has been a fantastic friend and sister to me. She has every right to feel angry, disappointed, and betrayed. She is right. I let this happen. I was trying to protect Ash instead of confronting the truth. I'm not bailing Ash out of any more situations she

created. I have to let her be the fuck up she is so desperately trying to become. She doesn't cook, clean, have a talent, possess a trade, and refuses to get a job or education. She truly believes she can survive this world with her looks and body. No shade, no cap, little sis is a baddie, but Bitch it's an apocalypse of every woman being fine and cute. If they're not fine today, they will be next year when their taxes hit. Ash, little sister, get your shit together! You're a dime a dozen in this 21st-century market of building a body. Men are looking to build empires and generational wealth. A woman creates that with ambition and execution, not a pretty face and body. A lot of women want the crown without the labour. Sis! Nah, you're hustling backwards. There is no better feeling than writing and cashing your own checks. That's the real black girl luxury. I should have listened when CJ first warned me to let the cat out of the bag. *Wait. Now that I think about it, how can she talk? Why the fuck didn't she tell Mia when she found out? This emotionless bitch created the term "sneaky link" in layman's terms... creeping. The main reason she doesn't like Ray is she's his identical twin in female form.*

But at least she's single! She wouldn't know commitment if it personally dick slapped her in the crotch. I'm still trying to figure out why nobody is talking about CJ pulling a gun on Ray. I wish she would have popped his ass. Oh, and I see Ava with the shits. She's playing sides but claiming she is neutral and not in it. *Yes, bitch, you're in it the moment you spoke your two cents. How about you clean around your own front porch first before you try cleaning mine?* Poor Brandi. Ava is about to keep wasting her fucking time. She knows damn well she doesn't want to marry Brandi. Instead of facing her demons, she chooses to bury them in other women's souls. *Ava, honey, stop calling the pot black. You are a female fuck boy. You know, the narcissistic, impulsive, I don't want to be alone kind. Grow up bitch!*

Liv, you barely missed the chopping block. Only because you are busy dealing with your shit as you should. Hear this bitch and hear it loud. You're about to ruin things with Patrick with your Olivia syndrome. Everything is not centered around you and your terms and your success. Do you understand why it's called partnership and not individual-ship? Put that independent shit in a jar and use it as needed. Patrick is a once-in-a-lifetime kind of guy. He cares for Ryan as if she's his own. He is handsome, honest, stable, goal-oriented, intelligent, thoughtful, and kind. He always comes through not only for you, but also for the people around you. We learned to give and take –compromise– when we were five. Sis. I talk all this shit, and I have just as many issues as these bitches. With my insecurity, I'm desperate to be with a boss, looking ass. I still check all of Eric's social media platforms, and he is married with a child. Yea, bitch, you're desperate! Let us not forget I fucked him 30 days after his wedding. Oh well, it was my dick first, and that was my parting gift. Now, I never said we're not in contact anymore. I allow him to send me messages to my DM. I entertain them when I'm bored. That's the only way he can reach me since I blocked his ass off my phone. This hoe ass nigga is so bold and disrespectful; he had the nerve to send me a plane ticket to Turks and Caicos last week. Boy, FUCK You! Take that weak-ass bitch you settled for.

If she was what you truly wanted, you wouldn't still be coming for me. The fuck! One thing I've learned to be a very true statement, "you teach people how to treat you or settle for what they give you!" I'm no longer accepting broken promises and apologies with no changed behaviour, nor will I abide by society or these niggas' standards. I'm riding my own wave. Women nowadays have more significant dick energy than men. We have to train them to use a tool they were born with. Most little boys learned to pee standing up from a woman, their mom. They quickly forget that tidbit when they experience their first nut. I remember reading the U S Census Bureau report that 18.4 million boys were born without a father. Are we still wondering why the men aren't men-ing? Bitch, they don't know how to be a man. Single mothers raise them, and they grow up thinking they can tell a woman how to be in her essence when, in reality, they need to be groomed into men. Yea, Ms. Pat, it's your fault Lil James is full of shit, entitled, and emotionally challenged. You raised him to be the man you wanted as a woman instead of teaching and training him on how to be a responsible man. How to be a man of his word. "One that says what he means and means what he says." How to clean up after himself, work hard, chivalry; you know, good character traits. I know we ladies get offended when we're told our sons need their fathers or male role models. I'm sorry to be the messenger, it's true! He does! We're equipped to do many things, and we can raise young boys, but we CAN NOT teach them how to be a man. We weren't born in that species. We don't even have identical chromosomes. There are some things we, as women, don't identify within the male species. A man instills those things in young boys. I didn't say we weren't capable. I'm just saying that as a woman, we're frustrated with these fuck boys because of their female traits. *He got that from Ms. Pat, Sis!* She taught him that. Introduce them young boys to sports, being around other young men, barbershops, happily married men, and fathers. Men in the church who understand who God truly is because who wants a man that doesn't pray for her, anyway? *We're tired of raising y'all sons, Ms. Pat!* Chile, I have exhausted myself with this rant. I need to recap and recoup! Wine me, please! And roll me up while you are at it. I'm Sharice Ryan, better known as Reece, and these are my sisters, my thoughts, my truth, and the first chapter of my story.....

Made in the USA
Las Vegas, NV
05 September 2022

54648947R00088